MY EDUCATION

CREATION OF THE HOMUNCULUS II

MY
EDUCATION

— ❧ *A*
Book of ❧ —
Dreams

WILLIAM S.
BURROUGHS

VIKING

VIKING
Published by the Penguin Group
Penguin Books USA Inc., 375 Hudson Street, New York, New York 10014, U.S.A.
Penguin Books Ltd, 27 Wrights Lane, London W8 5TZ, England
Penguin Books Australia Ltd, Ringwood, Victoria, Australia
Penguin Books Canada Ltd, 10 Alcorn Avenue,
Toronto, Ontario, Canada M4V 3B2
Penguin Books (N.Z.) Ltd, 182-190 Wairau Road,
Auckland 10, New Zealand

Penguin Books Ltd, Registered Offices:
Harmondsworth, Middlesex, England

First published in 1995 by Viking Penguin,
a division of Penguin Books USA Inc.

3 5 7 9 10 8 6 4 2

Photograph of Michael Emerton on page 191, © James Grauerholz
Frontispiece illustration, "Creation of the Homunculus II,"
by William S. Burroughs.

LIBRARY OF CONGRESS CATALOGING IN PUBLICATION DATA
Burroughs, William S.
My education: a book of dreams/William S. Burroughs.
p.   cm.
ISBN 0–670–81350–8
1. Creation (Literary, artistic, etc.)—Fiction. 2. Dreams—Fiction.
I. Title.
PS3552.U75M9   1994
813'.54–dc20
94–10342

This book is printed on acid-free paper.

Printed in the United States of America
Set in Bodoni Book
Designed by Brian Mulligan

TO MICHAEL EMERTON
January 18, 1966–November 4, 1992

I haunted the city of your dreams, invisible and insistent as a fire of thorns in the wind.

—St.-John Perse, *Anabasis*

ACKNOWLEDGMENTS

My thanks to Jim McCrary, who over a period of several years carefully transcribed these texts from many hastily jotted notes on scraps of paper and index cards and pages typed with one hand. Thanks also to David Ohle, who did some of that transcription; to James Grauerholz, who maintained the ever-growing folders of raw typescript as they accumulated, and who reviewed and edited the final work; and to David Stanford, who patiently prodded and encouraged me in the completion of this book.

MY EDUCATION

Airport. Like a high school play, attempting to convey a spectral atmosphere. One desk onstage, a gray woman behind the desk with the cold waxen face of an intergalactic bureaucrat. She is dressed in a gray-blue uniform. Airport sounds from a distance, blurred, incomprehensible, then suddenly loud and clear. "Flight sixty-nine has been—" Static . . . fades into the distance . . . "Flight . . ."

Standing to one side of the desk are three men, grinning with joy at their prospective destinations. When I present myself at the desk, the woman says: "You haven't had your education yet."

This dream occurred approximately thirty-five years ago, shortly after the publication of *Naked Lunch* with the Olympia Press in Paris in 1959.

Recall a cartoon in *The New Yorker,* years ago: Four men with drinks, at a table, and one insisting on telling a dream he dreamed:

"You were in it, too, Al, and you were a little white dog with an Easter bonnet. Ha ha ha . . . Now isn't that funny?" Al doesn't think so. He looks like he would ram a broken glass into the dreamer's mouth, if he wasn't a neutered male in a *New Yorker* cartoon.

For years I wondered why dreams are so often so dull when related, and this morning I find the answer, which is very simple—like most answers, you have always known it: *No context . . .* like a stuffed animal set on the floor of a bank.

The conventional dream, approved by the psychoanalyst, clearly, or by obvious association, refers to the dreamer's waking life, the people and places he knows, his desires, wishes, and obsessions. Such dreams radiate a special disinterest. They are as boring and as commonplace as the average dreamer. There is a special class of dreams, in my experience, that are not dreams at all but quite as real as so-called waking life and, in the two examples I will relate, completely unfamiliar as regards my waking experience but, if one can specify degrees of reality, more real by the impact of unfamiliar scenes, places, personnel, even odors.

The two non-dreams are also unique in my dream experience. They are both flying dreams but unlike other flying dreams I have experienced. In most flying dreams I find a high cliff or building and soar off knowing that this is a dream and I won't fall and kill myself. In another flying dream I flap my arms and manage with some effort to attain an altitude of fifteen or twenty feet. In a third type I am jet-propelled at great speed across the sky. In the two dreams that follow I find myself *lighter than air.* I float up, airborne, controlling both direction and speed.

I'm in a room with a high ceiling and a door at one end. The room is full of light and has a feeling of being open and airy. I float up to the ceiling and bob along to the door and out. There is a porch or balcony over the room and now I am up under the porch about thirty feet off the ground. I move out from under the porch and pick up speed and direction.

I land in a catwalk open to my left. Walking down, I see a door at the end of the walkway, about six feet wide and eight feet high. Outside the door a boy in a gray sweatsuit is working at something I can't see, with his back to me. I feel he is hostile, and I couldn't care less. The door opens and a man emerges. He is wearing a very dark blue striped suit, with a tie. He has a black mustache. He looks at me without a trace of friendliness or hostility. Just registering my presence. No one I ever saw before. Out to my left there is a ditch about thirty feet below the ramp where I am standing. Beyond that some pine trees and what looks like a cemetery . . . mausoleums with inscriptions embossed in white stone . . .

Had I gone down there (sorry—time to wake up . . .) I might have found my own name in stone relief, like the stained-glass window in a church in Citronelle, Alabama:

SACRED TO THE MEMORY OF
WILLIAM SEWARD BURROUGHS

My grandfather, whom of course I never saw, died here in Citronelle, of tuberculosis, aged forty-one.

The beautiful mausoleum is empty.

The city is gray and the streets are empty. I am standing in front of a hotel and I can see down to an intersection and some billboards on a brick wall. The only light in the city is directly in front of the hotel, a splash of yellow, a compromise implicit in the concept of a hotel: a place for travelers from places where there is yellow light. Like a bar in a Moslem country. The physicists tell us that nothing can exceed the speed of light . . .

Perhaps this is a place that doesn't enter the race. A neutral timeless space-less place of shadows. I can levitate because there is no gravity here. This is then a place at the other end of the spectrum from a black hole where gravity holds even light in its immeasurably impacted weight. I find that I can levitate right off the sidewalk in front of the hotel *and I know this is not a dream,* that I am really floating up off the ground, and gaining speed now above the hotel, which is five stories tall—I'm five hundred feet above the sidewalk. I come back down in front of the hotel, and the streets are still empty and nobody sees me. Then a fattish woman with a short-sleeved dress, so her upper arms are bare, is going into the hotel and I nudge her with my foot but she doesn't see me. I alight in front of the hotel entrance and follow her in and her husband comes out of a room in back of the lobby. He is a Weather Cop. I tell him someone nudged his wife because her arms are bare and people here are very puritanical. He accepts this and I go up to my room on the fifth floor. The ceiling is metal tin stamp, printed in circular patterns painted white, like you still see in old hotels and cafeterias, and the bed is narrow and has iron bedsteads painted dark brown. I float up and hit the ceiling, and I can see the patterns stamped on the tin. Then I come back down and up and in front of a mirror, but when I levitate I can't see my image in the mirror. Then a maid comes in with a carafe of some yellowish liquid and a jug of hot liquid. I say I didn't order anything, but it is a courtesy of the hotel. The liquids give off a sour chemical smell that is definitely unpleasant. Then a *very* ugly woman comes in with a bulbous forehead and fat arms and a pushed-in face really *hideous*. Then two men come in and begin tinkering with an electrical contrivance attached to the foot of the bed. Something like an air conditioner, but it looks old-fashioned and out of repair.

The smell that came out of the carafe and the pitcher—no way I can exactly place it. A sour chemical smell that also came off that ugly woman, and in fact permeates the room and the hotel. Maybe it came from the electrical apparatus attached to the foot of the bed. It was an inorganic smell and at the same time a sour rotten smell, like bad air.

Going out the window to attend a performance I'd seen advertised on a billboard, and someone tells me that show isn't here yet. It's another show on now. I forget the name. I am afraid I will wake up in this bed and find that this is just a dream. Then I wake up in my bed in Lawrence and I realize that the dream in the gray, empty city is more real than my real life here in Lawrence.

There are some aliens camped near us in blue denim suits—Martians, I think—and I visit them. They seem friendly enough and one man takes off his clothes and there is a column of bone running down from his neck and nothing else except his hipbones. He says, "Well, I really got a turkey of a body . . ."

He shit sure does.

I feel heat in my foot and look down and there is a lighted cigarette shoved under the sole of my shoe near the toe. Someone has given me a hot foot. When I extract the cigarette, I break it open and it is like a clamshell with tentacles inside. Not however moving or alive.

Thoughts that arise palpable as a haze from the pages of Jean Genet's *Prisoner of Love.*

I have never felt close to any cause or people, so I envy from a distance of incomprehension those who speak of "my people." Jews, blacks, Palestinians, Chinese . . . But to affiliate myself with any such aggregate would be an act of brazen dilettantism that I could not begin to carry off. I would be immediately seen as an impostor and categorized as a spy. They would see through the sham at once. I am the worst of all liars, not through any principles of integrity, but through a basic disability. Lies just are not in me and neither is the truth. I could never have been a politician or a swindler, and of all people the most basically antagonistic are the WASPs with whom I was raised.

Ivy Lee, public relations expert for the Rockefeller family, was my uncle. And he hated me at first sight. His son James still refers to me as *"that* son of a bitch!"* in the same tone as the Israelis speak of Dr. Mengele because they never succeeded in finding him. Mendel, or is it Mengle? I can never get names straight. Why? *Because I have no name.* And the arbiters of destiny decided that I would not be allowed to profit from an assumed name. My last bequest from the Burroughs estate was $10,000. And very welcome at the time.

Genet is concerned with betrayal, to me a meaningless concept, like patriotism. I have nothing and nobody to betray and in consequence I am incorrigibly honest.

My criminal activities (minimal to be sure) were as hopelessly inept as my efforts to hold a job in an advertising agency or any other regular job.

Ted Morgan's biography starts with a basic misconception: *Literary Outlaw*. To be an outlaw you must first have a base in law to reject and get out of. I never had such a base. I never had a place I could call home that meant any more than a key to a house, apartment, or hotel room. This position or lack of position is incomprehensible to a French aristocrat like Sanche de Gramont. For the aristocrat is formed, limited, and defined by a little piece of earth that he is *from*. The aristocrat, the land*owner*, even more than the peasant who tills the land. The farmer can leave the land. The aristocrat may change his name but he will always carry the earth inside him. Speaking of black holes, Sanche said: "I would have to know what the cuisine is like." And I thought, "You are really earthbound." Cuisine! The aliens that have been contacted it seems have no stomachs.

Am I an alien? Alien from what exactly? Perhaps my home is the dream city, more real than my so-called waking life precisely because it has no relation to waking life. In the hotel room I was afraid I would wake up and find it was all a dream, my ability to levitate, *but I was afraid of waking up in that bed in that hotel room, not in my room here in Lawrence.* A gray haze permeates the city and there is no discernible light source, but I can see a reasonable distance. A twilight haze that has no relation to time of day. *In fact there is no time here.* The hideous woman who came into my room was always hideous, she did not get that way from age and length of time.

Brion Gysin was the only man I have ever respected. One of the attributes that I respected was his unfailing and dazzling tact, which is one reason why he was blocked and distrusted by the haute monde. He had no *right* to outdo them *in manners*. But the "socially prominent" have insulated themselves from the source of tact, which is discernment and perception. Meeting a stranger he, or more likely she, will immediately try to determine the stranger's "social position." There is no more degrading force than snobbery, the female principle at its cruel and bitchy worst. How Mrs. Worldly loves to see Mr. Unsuitable squirm as she, with a few words in just the right tone . . . "What was that name again?" . . . conveys "social inferiority" or, with just a slightly lifted eyebrow and an almost imperceptible recoil: "Ghastly creeping creature, how did you creep into my drawing room?"

This hideous disease of the spirit still poisons the air of England and was eagerly imported in the 1890s by the Four Hundred. A goodly portion went down with the *Titanic*. Mr. Vanderbilt, or someone of his ilk, and his valet put on full dress suits and said: "We are going down like gentlemen." But an Italian steward put on women's clothes and scuttled into the first lifeboat, and Colonel Clinch Smith, an old soldier, latched onto a chicken coop and survived.

And that's the name of the game here on Planet Earth. While I admire the dazzling innocence of the antihero—the ship's captain who puts on women's clothes and rushes into the first lifeboat—in an actual emergency, I would probably react with exemplary selflessness, taking, that is, the easy way—easy for one who has no clearly delineated self to put before every other consideration.

Genet is concerned with betrayal. I have nothing and nobody to betray, *moi*. In *Prisoner of Love* a perceptive black officer from Sudan named Mubarak says to Genet: "The Israeli soldiers are young. Would you be glad to be with them? I expect they would be very nice to you."

As for *moi* it would make little difference to me which side I was with. (*With,* not *on.*) I can see value in both. But when it comes to the situation in South Africa there is for me only one side possible. Why don't the blacks wise up and start using chemical and biological weapons? Imagine a potion that would turn the whites black like the white in Johannesburg who was stung by bees, swelled up and turned black, so they took him to the Nigger Hospital and he wakes up screaming: "Where am I, you black bastards?"

And here, you young lions, is a recipe for making botulism, used with conspicuous success by Pancho Villa against the federal troops in Mexico:

Fill a water canteen to the top with freshly cooked and drained green beans. Close it and put aside for several days. A few slivers of rotting pork are then added, and the canteen sealed tightly. Ten incubators are buried underground. After seven days most will be swollen, indicating a thriving botulism culture.

Can be smeared on any fruit, meats, or vegetables, dabbed on thornbushes and fragments of glass. Guerrilla children sniped sentries with pottery shards or with obsidian chips dipped in botulism. A little ingenuity. There are many ways and it takes such a *little* to do the Big Job. A woman opened a can of home-canned beans. Put one bean in her mouth, spit it out and washed her mouth out with mouthwash. She died three days later from botulism poisoning.

Packing dreams can also be called time dreams, since packing and journeys are always concerned with time. Too little time and too much to pack. Every drawer or closet I open overflows with articles that must be packed into suitcases too small to hold them. Then another drawer, another closet with clothes spilling out. A gathering tension in the groin that may culminate in orgasm. Wet dreams, in my experience, often have no overt sexual context. For example, two or three years ago in Los Angeles I was on a train station platform with Antony Balch (who was already dead at the time). The train is pulling out and I am running diagonally towards it. Train gathering speed. Will I make it? Wake up ejaculating. In Egyptian hieroglyphs the ejaculating phallus is used in various non-sexual contexts. It can mean "to stand up in evidence," "before or in the presence of," or "before" in the time sense.

The orgasm in packing dreams can be interpreted as an ejaculation of compressed time. Last night I had a packing dream in reverse. I can't find my black zipper suitcase. (Not surprising since I don't own such an article.) Every closet and every drawer I open is *empty*. Now there are two women in my hotel room with old-style surveying instruments like the beautifully designed brass telescopes and navigation instruments you see in certain antique stores. I see now a small pistol built like a watch of brass with long thin bullets of no known caliber. Obviously I can't take it through customs, so I deny ownership. Wake up without an erection. Packing dream has been canceled like matter and antimatter. An interesting question is raised in evidence: *Does sex have anything to do with sex?* The whole ritual of sex, courtship, desire itself, the panting and sweating and positions, a sham, while the actual buttons are pushed offstage?

As if one goes through a complex ceremony to produce light then someone else, at a given moment, flicks the light switch. Why does the packing or time dream evoke orgasm in a man over seventy? There is perhaps as intimate a relation between time and sex as between death and sex. Both death and sex *take the subject out of time.*

The Land of the Dead can be identified by certain signs: The people are all dead and known to me, Mother, Dad, Mort, Brion Gysin, Ian Sommerville, Antony Balch, Michael Portman (Mikey), Kells Elvins. There is always difficulty in obtaining breakfast or any food for that matter. The set is usually some section, three or four blocks of Paris, Tangier, London, New York, St. Louis. And what is outside this dreary claustrophobic area? What lies beyond the Expanding Universe? Answer: Nothing. But??? No but. That is all you-I-they . . . can see or experience with their senses, their telescopes, their calculations.

According to John Wheeler and his Recognition Physics, nothing exists until it is observed by a "meaning sensitive observer." Well, certainly not for the observer. How could it exist for him until he observes it? But he also has to pin it down, record it on some instrument or other. In order to get itself observed and so to exist, the as yet unconceived instance or being must exert a *measurable effect*. It does seem that these physicists go to some effort and expense to state what seems obvious. How can you measure something that occasions no effect on anything?

In Hamburg a priest is smoking opium. A cobblestone alley with horse manure. End of the line, waiting for the Saint Patrick Special back to town.

"Like other leaders he stood up the instant a fedayeen came into Arafat's office. The fighter, bringing in a newspaper, a telegram, a cup of coffee or a pack of cigarettes, was bound to know what it meant: If you're a hero you are as good as dead so we render to you a funeral tribute. We've got springs under our seats and as soon as a hero comes in, we are ejected into mourning."

What a writer and what a meaning sensitive observer. "I grovel in admiration." This phrase I lift from a book where some behind-the-lines Scotch-drinking PLO speaks of a girl who will ride a donkey loaded with explosives into Israeli lines. It occurred to me that prostrate groveling would be a wise procedure for anyone in the vicinity of this admirable act.

Genet returns to the story of the Cid, who kissed the leper. Now leprosy is one of the least contagious of diseases, so the saintly Cid was in no danger of infection. Bring me a leper and I will kiss it.

Genet continues: "There are still two or three hospitals that look after lepers. But do they really look after them? Perhaps experts inject people with the virus so that future Cids can show what heroism and charity an Arab is capable of."

Hansen's bacillus is not a virus but a relatively large rod-shaped bacillus very similar to *Bacillus* Koch TB. It is transmitted by long, close contact, sharing sheets and towels. A pestiferous Christian missionary I met in Pucallpa, Peru, said leprosy was passed by sexual intercourse . . . to quote him: "I can't think of a more likely way to catch it."

This missionary told me he wanted to see a law against Yage "with teeth in it," and he bared his teeth in a most offensive manner, taking the law into his own Spam-eating mouth. After thirty-seven years I hate him at this moment, 9:06 a.m., Tuesday, October 23, 1990.

Perhaps he would forgive me and love me if given the chance extraordinary across time like a literal Christian. ("Brother, we teach them the Bible!") But he never knew me as an enemy. Such people hold intuition in horror.

"The word of God says the Occult is the enemy."

Survival is the name of the game, William. The scruffiest hippie is my messenger . . . do not expect radiant messengers of light. Expect the flawed, the maimed in body and spirit. It's all a film run backward . . . the Atom Bomb through the Manhattan Project to the formula . . . $E = MC^2$.

"We should have occupied every place."

A sword with a clock in the side. A nudist party.

(Vivarium floats in hiatus. Beautiful snake, very venomous. It *looks* deadly, a dazzling, shiny white with brilliant red spots.)

I climb to the top floor of a vast warehouse by iron stairs and ramps, a big bare room with windows I can look five hundred feet down. I have come here, of course, to soar down. Need something to break out a window. An iron bar or perhaps a barstool—like the man who broke a glass door in the Milky Way in Amsterdam and Benn Posset shielded me with his body?

I am in my pajamas at a discontinued subway stop.

Now with James Grauerholz rushing through subway stations with inhuman speed and agility. Jumping across tracks, down stairways, floating through turnstiles . . . and here we are at Johnson's store, open-air booths with counters on four sides.

So here I am in the Land of the Dead with Mikey Portman. We are sharing an apartment which consists of two rooms with a bathroom between them. Mikey's room is also provided with a sleeping porch. There are two beds side by side and touching each other, lumpy-looking mattresses, throw rugs, eiderdowns, cushions covered in tattered, frayed yellow and gold velvet. Looks like the madam's room in a whorehouse, lacking only an asthmatic Pekingese. It seems an old German lady with tight lace collar and high-button, black shoes has been billeted on us for the night.

Mikey is on the sleeping porch wrapped up in a pink blanket. I tell him he should let her sleep on one of the beds. After all, he can retire to the sleeping porch. And I have assurances she will not even remove her clothes.

"No, I don't want her in here."

"Well, you can stay on the porch. There are two beds."

"I might want to sleep in here."

No use. Death hasn't changed him a bit; the same selfish, self-centered, spoiled, petulant, weak Mikey Portman.

Now I see a small black dog peeking out of the bathroom door, which is ajar . . . dog all black, shiny black . . . with a long pointed muzzle quivering like a dowser wand.

"Where did that door dog come from? What is it doing here?"

"Does it matter?" Distilled concentrate of petulant Portman.

"Door man . . . door dog," I say.

He doesn't answer. Obviously I will have to billet the old German lady in my room, which is a duplicate of his room except the beds are smaller.

On a plane and it is going down and I know this is *reality*.

No feeling of a dream . . . we are going down. Passengers across the aisle are all standing up now to see something I can't see because they block my view.

However, the plane lands safely and we disembark on a city street that looks like the Main in Montréal.

"I'm a dreamer Montréal?"

A painting tells a story but viewed from different time and positions simultaneously. Cézanne shows a pear seen close up, at a distance, from various angles and in different light . . . the pear at dawn, midday, twilight . . . all compacted into one pear . . . time and space in a pear, an apple, a fish. Still life? No such thing. As he paints, the pear is ripening, rotting, shrinking, swelling.

An example from my own painting: A flooded, washed-out bridge seen from the side. An approaching truck seen head-on from a distance, the moment when the driver sees that the bridge is gone, a close-up of his face, the fear and calculations written on his face as he unhooks the seat belt. Applies the brakes. All happening at the same time so far as the viewer is concerned.

Take a picture by Brion Gysin: "Outskirts of Marrakech." Phantom motor scooters and bicycles. Solid scooters and bicycles. A place the painter had been many times at many different times. As he walks he sees a scooter from yesterday, last year. Perhaps from tomorrow as well, since he is painting from a *position above time.*

And so dreams tell stories, many stories. I am writing a story, if it could be so called, about the *Mary Celeste.* I am painting scenes from the story I am writing. And I am dreaming about the *Mary Celeste,* the dreams feeding back into my writing and painting. A burst of fresh narrative: the Celestial Babies and the Azore Islands . . . digression and parentheses, other data seemingly unrelated to the saga of the *Mary Celeste,* now another flash of story . . . a long parenthesis. Stop. Change. Start.

Should I tidy up, put things in a rational sequential order? *Mary Celeste* data together? Flying dreams together? Land of the Dead dreams together? Packing dreams together? To do so would involve a return to the untenable position of an omniscient observer in a timeless vacuum. But the observer is observing other data, associations flashing backward and forward.

For example, I just remembered a dream where I met a man called Slim I allegedly knew thirty years ago in London. Slim? I don't remember. Thirty years ago? A dull ache . . . "old unhappy far-off things" . . . I meet Slim at the doorway of some apartment. What does he look like? Gray, anonymous face dimmed out of focus? What is he wearing? Gray suit, gray tie, suggestion of scarf and a watch chain.

You see, I am seeing him as he was thirty years ago, five years ago, yesterday, today . . . like Brion's motor scooter in Marrakech. So I should put Slim back there in the paragraph about Brion's Marrakech painting? I don't think so. Who runs can read.

New York City dawn streets. Making my way from downtown back to my hotel in the 50s. Yes, I can feel the key in my pocket. A market where a number of people are emptying garbage bags. A truck is unloading the bags. Someone has found a gun. What a fool to turn it in, I think. Up on the top floor of a high building I can see down a narrow air shaft, pipes and iron ladders five hundred feet down. Why walk? I jump off an iron balcony and swim through the air uptown.

Meet two naked angels about sixteen. They say it's their first solo flight. The city spread out underneath us about a thousand feet down, in beautiful pastel shades . . . all quite idyllic. I acquire some liquid nourishment in a silver trough. It is creamy and custardy and it tastes delicious . . . I absorb some by a sort of osmosis. (Reminds me of a recent dream in Tangier cafe and various old friends turn up. Old friends like Slim whom I don't remember seeing before, but who are nonetheless familiar.)

The proprietor brings out a bar like a gold ingot, about eight inches long and brown on the outside. He cuts off one side and inside is a creamy filling . . . looks like crème brûlée, clearly delicious and I am eating it with my *eyes*. It's known as *Eye Candy* . . . breathing it in through my eyes. (As a child of three I thought that one saw with one's mouth. My brother then told me to close my eyes and open my mouth and I got the idea that I couldn't see with my mouth . . . but people do *feast* their eyes.) So, still carrying this silver trough, I alight with the two angelic boys on a balcony where Colonel Massek of the advertising firm Van Dolen, Givordan and Massek, where I worked in 1942, is now located. He, the Colonel, says I can go out for lunch. I tell him I've already eaten. The balcony is a thousand feet above the city . . . stunning view.

"Well," I say, "let's go."

One of the boys says he has "lost it" and it is a long way down. As a test I raise myself three feet off the floor, but none of the kids in the office seem to notice anything, so I take off into what I now call "*my* element," out through the clouds, and in fact sit down on a cloud, which I can do because I got no weight at all. Just floating, lonely as a cloud, and the view is so breathtaking and no fear of falling anymore. I got no body to fall. Just me and my shadow. Strolling down the avenue over New York.

There is no hurry . . . no hurry at all.

Being conceived is like you are in a car driven by the father . . . faster, faster, faster . . . only this time it is Mother who was driving when we crashed and in the time it took the hydraulic brakes to take hold, I had written out two hundred pages of images . . . poetic images yet. But I know it was only two pages and that is the way people talk here. They exaggerate by a hundred, like putting bigger numbers on the money.

Then I'm in a room with Ian who looks all pink and red . . . a beautiful terra-cotta color . . . and these phantoms keep coming in, look like people but are just as fraudulent and if you shove them they disappear.

Quite a number of them came.

Mikey Portman and I have teamed up some way and we are photographs . . . and we say:

"We are photographs and we will turn everyone else into photographs."

There is a screaming child there and I am afraid to touch it to comfort it since I know it will bite me.

In a cafe mezzanine, Clarence Darrow is seated at a table. Brion and I introduce ourselves. Darrow looks very trim and youngish. A well-kept forty-five, in a gray suit. Darrow was a belt-and-braces atheist, said already he is losing his memory a piece at a time. "When I die," he says, "I won't be any more aware of my approaching extinction than an old log rotting in the woods." Well, speak for yourself, Clarence.

Any case, he is looking good. I notice that his thin mouth is almost at the end of his chin.

Out in the street I don't know how to find my way back. I have money for a cab, but I don't see any cabs and wouldn't in any case know where to tell him to go. I am looking for a place to have breakfast. If I could get to some familiar landmark. Is it Paris? . . . Land of the Dead, probably. Pass a crowded place on several levels like Le Drugstore, and there is a hotel restaurant. I see a small cafe and go in.

Three people behind zinc counter about three feet long and two patrons in tiny booths with coffee. The people behind the counter look dead, a gray-green color, like "The Absinthe Drinkers." There are two men and one woman. I don't know whether to sit down in a booth or get coffee at the counter. There is a stool at the end of the counter. I sit down and the stool is wobbly. I finally try another stool, which also wobbles, and the people behind the counter start laughing, and I walk out.

I see a man in a gray suit waiting by an orange sign I figure must be a streetcar stop but I don't know how to ask him for directions, not being sure of where I want to go. There is a hotel and another stop I need to make. Then I meet Brion Gysin and he says there is a hall in the vicinity where Allen and Huncke will read or have read. Then he leads the way down a long street . . . faster and faster. I see a clock: 6:10. We are moving always faster . . . now a blur of red painting, red faces from Renoir, red scarves, red geraniums . . . faster and faster . . . a blur of red . . .

A creature clearly humanoid about three feet in length. He had clear, enormous, pink eyes which then turned clear red. I touched his head and found he was burning with fever.

Moving through a maze of corridors and rooms, opening drawers and closets. There is a long corridor like a ship deck, open on one side, that ended in an enormous room with a ceiling of a certain wavy effect like in my painting, like beaten copper or silver. There is a table at which Brion was seated and a little boy with a black eye flew through the air and lighted on my lap.

In Mexico, I think. A cop accused me of being one of those who fired shots from a streetcar. He is leading me towards a huge steel door set in a concrete abutment, like a subway. I ask him to show me his badge. He says he doesn't have a badge because he speaks Spanish.

A dreary Antarctic city. Old tenement-like buildings . . . no one in sight. By a park with heavy trees some denizens of the city are butchering poultry.

I was in Tangier, sitting at the very back of the cafe in the Place de France, opposite the Cafe de France. As I sat there I saw Paul

Bowles walk out and turn left. Perhaps he was on his way to the taxi stand. There was a disturbance in the street. I saw a bloody machete and a uniformed policeman. Brion was there and he indicated that the man next to me was a detective. The man got very close. He was short, dressed all in black, with big, square, white teeth. A face like parchment and a look about his torso as if it were simply a frame of wood or metal around which his clothes were buttoned. He held his torso completely rigid, at all times balanced on short legs. It seems the incident involved a man who was drunk and who had attacked someone with the machete.

The plainclothes cop asked:

"Is he a junko as well?"

Then he walked away up a narrow alley. I met Achmed Jacoubi on the street and he took me up a flight of stairs to Brion's house. This was a small, square room on two levels. On each level was a bed. The lower-level bed was Brion's. An open arched door with a beaded curtain led to a terrace. I stepped through the curtain. The terrace is irregularly shaped and about thirty feet above street level. There is also an eight-foot wall along one side. The view is beautiful . . . pastel shades of blue and yellow. Opposite is a high building perched on a cliff some eighty feet above the street. A woman lowers a red bag of laundry on a rope from a balcony at the top of the cliff building.

Mikey Portman with an eerie little boy. The boy is quite small, not more than four feet tall, but somehow looking miniature rather than an ungrown child. His eyes are very large and bluish, but it's rather like the whole eye socket is large and pulls down, with lashes on top and the lower eyelid almost two inches below. Are the eyes blue or a deep blue-black, like a smear of color? He is fully dressed in

a white shirt and a sweater. We are, all three, in a bed under a
coverlet in what seems to be a dormitory.

Floor in a small side room of algae or green paint. On instructions I draw in two Taber guns on the floor.

A naked boy of seven is brought in on a stretcher. There is now
what looks like an operating table in the room. The boy has just
been "minted." His flesh is white and smooth as alabaster. Genitals
perfectly formed, but uncircumcised. I say he should be circum-
cised before leaving the hospital—that is, before the "reanimation."
A tarpaulin separates this room from another small room with a
shower. Now a beautiful boy of fifteen appears and we enter the
shower room together, moving the tarpaulin to one side. I notice he
has the same smooth, white, alabaster flesh. He is smiling, relaxed,
receptive.

I buy six caps of H from Old Dave. Bill Belli is there talking about
going to Chicago to hear a band. Find twenty dollars in my pocket
to buy the ten caps at two dollars each. He is selling out of room
141, just across the hall.

The room is small, completely unfurnished, no pictures on the
walls of a dingy, dirty white. Floors are cheap stained wood. At the
east end of the room is a small window one-third open. I can see a
wing of the same building projecting to my left, small windows,
dirty gray-yellow brick. I can see down a thousand feet to dingy
gray streets. Shall I open the window and jump down? The gray
emptiness blocks me. No color, no life anywhere, nothing but this
empty room. Looking out I can see no open spaces, just gray buildings and a narrow canyon down to the streets. I see a beam, a two-
by-four of yellow pine in a ray of light. It is a sign.

I open the window and dive down, falling with the dead weight of my body . . . faster . . . faster . . . WHOOSH. I explode out the sides, standing now in a gray street. I can fly up to thirty feet with considerable effort. I come to a wharf where old clipper ships are stacked against each other like stage props. Can they be made serviceable with magnetic sails that will drive the ship a hundred miles an hour?

"What is your hurry to get nowhere?"

Someone is with me now—a brother in the junkyard of dead tattered sails and wrecked ships.

A fog of pain and despair drifts on an iron-blue painted sea. Dead Time. The ships are crushed flat by the pressure of time, stacked against each other, leaning against a wooden stand.

An inlet around a promontory with cliffs thirty or so feet high. I walk around with someone to the side of a pond which is now full of fish. Mostly small, about eight inches. Now I see that there are some fish as long as a foot and they all have long, extended mouths like bills, coming to rather a sharp point. There is something repulsive and alien about these fish and I don't want to catch one. I say: "The pond fills up at high tide."

Antony Balch is with me and we have to catch a boat train at 1:24, or is it 2:24? My bag is all packed and I just have to put on my coat and walk out. There are about fifteen minutes left and Antony says: "South London is very expensive."

I am in a dark room where I can see my face in a mirror. It seems to be a metal mirror on a cabinet of some sort. My face is quite young, about eighteen, with a curious dark red color like faces in a painting I did today . . . dusky red and also scarred or damaged in some way around the mouth and chin. It may be some sort of skin eruption. There are several views—some quite close.

An old gray book with several stories. One story concerns the discovery of an ancient tablet, one side in the ancient script, the other side in Johnson English. The tablet looks like what I call "the Ancient Tablet."

John de C. with a paint knife and some yellowish paint.

A very realistic dream about a hotel in the Land of the Dead. All the doors are open. I am going somewhere and there are customs agents in the hotel room. Can't find my luggage. One very small suitcase in gray-color cloth. They open it and take out my single-action .45. It looks like bad trouble.

I walk out looking for breakfast. Is there room service? It seems not. The dining room is deserted . . . a few waiters sitting around but no sign of food.

A big party with caviar and all sort of fancy foods. Brion is there and Jacques Stern. Windup is I get no food.

Thursday. Day of the week I was born on, if my memory serves. I was trying to shave, on a stairway leading from a shower. John de C. comes out of the shower wrapped in a bath towel. In a metal mirror, the light uncertain, my face appears much younger, an eighteen-year-old face for shaving. (Is this the same face of dusky red color in one of my recent paintings? or was that another dream?) I find a piece of soap and lather my face. I will shave with the soap, but now I can't find my gold razor.

Wheeler Restaurant . . . very small . . . has the waitress seen the H&K 9mm in my holster under the coat?

Land of the Dead. No breakfast. No liquor. No dinner.

The old family ghost is in the front room connected to Ginger Cat, who just jumped off my bed and ran out there. I berate myself:

"Get out there you yellow bastard and confront it."

Fear is shameful. I go out. The cat squeezes under a wire fence that has replaced the front door and runs out. I can hear her mewling out there.

I walk out into bright silver moonlight, searing moonlight, the light of Margaras the White Cat. All hidden things are revealed in the light of the Hunting Cat. To my left I see harlequin figures clear and sharp in the white light.

Who is the ghost in the front room? How can I distance myself and confront it?

The answer to any question will be revealed when you stop asking questions and wipe from your mind the concept of question.

In a library someone throws an old book with a hard red cover on the floor. I pick it up and read the title: *The Happy Net.*

A big party in NYC. Ian is there and Anne Waldman, the Naropa Mother. You need a place to stay? You got a dose of clap? Take all your troubles to the Naropa Mother. She gives all the satisfaction. I find that I am junk-sick and someone can give me a shot of Jade. We retire to a sort of bathroom with a double partition. I am looking around for a tap and basin, maybe I will have to use water from the toilet, but he brings out ampules in a paper box with directions in green letters. So he takes out a big ampule full of green liquid, loads it into a syringe, and shoots it into my mainline at the elbow and my arm swells up and turns purple like when I took the Bogomolets Anti-Human Serum—supposed to make me live to be 125—and I come near getting put in isolation in Panama, where the customs agent didn't half like the look of my arm. I tell him it is just an allergy.

I do notice a distinct sensation as this Jade drains all the way in. Not like junk, more like an injection of stone. Anyhow, stoned, but it isn't pleasant . . . Lots of people around and each one looks like the other and they have brought some *horrible* food . . . like raw entrails. This food is gross and there is a nightmare feeling here. Can't find Ian. Don't know how to get home or where home is.

Huncke's voice loud and clear—9:58 p.m.

At school in England. School is bare and spartan and there are only a handful of students, depending on how big your hand is. The Supervisor is thin and dedicated and *very* English. He is conscientious and trying to find digs for the students, of which there are very few, as I said. I see an apathetic brown dog and a few cats.

James is injured and immobilized, the flesh on his face looks slack and dead. I hear the Supervisor lives a very lonely and dedicated life. His wife is called Sally Sincere and that is enough to make any man lonely . . . by preference.

Ah yes . . . find some old dream notes in *Jaguar Woman* by Lynn Andrews. The Supervisor is connected to, or perhaps is, Fielding from *A Passage to India,* one of those very decent English types with a dim view of life and death.

Anything after death?

"I'm afraid not!" Fielding says.

Dolce Vita party in Italy. Plenty of fancy foods and a man with a huge gun. I say there will be support for Inspired Adventure.

"What sort of support?" Brion asks sharply.

"Rape and pillage. Better than nothing."

I am using myself as a reference point of view to assess current and future trends. This is not megalomania. It is simply the only measuring artifact available. Observer William: 023. Trends can be compacted into one word . . . GAP. Widening GAPs. GAP between 023 and those who can club seal cubs to death, set cats on fire, shoot out the eyes of lemurs with slingshots. (Oh sure, they are poor and hungry. From 023 they can get poorer and hungrier: 023 doesn't care if they starve to death. There is no empathy, no common ground.) Those who say: "I think animals are a splendid tool for research." . . . Most of it quite useless. But so it does save lives. *Human* lives. Too many already . . . 023 doesn't care. He contributes to Greenpeace, the Primate Center at Duke University, to "no-kill" animal shelters. Not a dime for cancer research!

GAP between 023 and antidrug hysterics like Daryl Gates, Chief of Police of Los Angeles, who says casual pot users should be taken out and shot, and someone named Davey in an article in *SWAT:* "All drug dealers, no matter how young, should be summarily executed. They are murderers many times over." (Like cigarette companies?) In the same category are Paki bashers, queer bashers, and anyone with a "Kill a Queer for Christ" sticker on his heap.

Nigger killers, raw material for lynch mobs, the Bible Belt, the fundamental Muslims—023 feels nothing for these specimens. GAP.

World leaders catering to the stupid and the bigoted. Bush says the drug war has united us as a nation. Of finks and lunatics? What do they care what someone else does in his own room? No skin off them.

GAP. 023 don't like liars. And lying comes natural as breathing to a politician.

The leaders are desperately trying to achieve a standard and malleable human product. But instead, by enforced proximity, the irreconcilable differences of interest and basic orientation are constantly reinforced and aggravated.

Fact is Homo Sap is fracturing into subspecies: 023 predicts that this trend of separation will continue and escalate and will be reflected in basic *biological differences* rather sooner than later.

The leaders, cut off from any intelligent and perceptive observers, will lose control. The motions they go through, the convergences and agreements, will have less and less relation to actual events. This is already happening in Russia. Another trend that will continue and escalate geometrically.

The violent bigots will become more and more bestial, degenerating into a hideous subspecies of vicious and graceless baboons.

"We know our duty."

"Vast army of purple-assed baboons."

The scientists will continue to reject the evidence with regard to ESP and UFOs and withdraw into academic vacuums.

GAP. GAP. GAP.

An earthquake in New York City. Brion was here. "Caught in New York beneath the animals of the Village. The Piper pulled down the sky."

I can read the minds of my enemies on TV. The bland lying faces like Larry Speakes, White House spokesman.

White House. White Wash.

James and I set out for a special restaurant in Mexico City. A batch of people sitting outside the restaurant. Now and again a number is called out.

Hotel room. A number of cats in a corridor and a large animal like a badger with coarse gray-brown hair.

My bed is full of cats. A mauve cat with green eyes, about four months old, is up by the pillow, and a little black kitten who bites and scratches. Two miniature cats fall into a bidet full of water. I bring them out. Wake up in dream and write down the dream.

In Paris with the dream notes. I see Ian across a wide street— gather my notes to cross. It takes a long time and by the time I can get across the street with heavy traffic, he is gone.

I go through a doorway into a courtroom. People are talking

French and they don't see me. Walk along a wide corridor and come to a coatroom, where I meet Ian. We embrace—and walk together. He turns into a cat. I walk on and come to a long glass case. There is a five-hundred-foot drop to a railroad station. I am about to jump off and sail down. Start to push the case over. Wake up and write the dream down.

At Price Road. Other people in the room. I open two capsules and rub shampoo in my hair. It is sticky. Mother comes in. We embrace and I tell her I love her. I go in the bathroom to wash the shampoo out. Stew Meyer is there. I decide to take a bath. There is a Vietnam vet in the bathroom who has been shot through the top of the head. The bullet (.223) came out his side. His face is strangely twisted with thick lips. He is still suffering from the effects of the wound.

I have to pack.

Looking for a place to have breakfast. Dining room with plates, bread and butter. Am I too late? It is ten past ten a.m. Others come in. With someone I go into the kitchen, find a birthday cake.

I'd eat anything at this point.

I am in Piccadilly. It is all so depressing I just want to go home. But I can't find my way. I am walking in narrow twisted streets like an Arab city. Shall I have a drink in a bar before going home? I look around and see what looks like a Greek bar and restaurant. An Arab boy strikes up a conversation. Clearly a propositional approach. We come to a room with a dance floor and people sitting at tables. I want to get out and go home. I start down a stairway hoping to lose the boy. I ask a man connected with the bar which is the way out. He points down the stairway and says: "Voilà."

Go with Felicity to an Arab bar to find my glasses, which are lost somewhere. Brion is dropping money on the floor. I am picking some of it up. "With my toes? Send someone down here!"

I meet a pale boy with a very large front tooth, very white and chipped half across.

A strange memory of a tennis court conveys a feeling of final desolation. Nothing there but the tennis court.

"Gone! All gone!"

Brion is there. And Ian.

I am in an earthquake somewhere. Things are shaking in the room and I don't know how bad the quake is. Now pictures are shaking on the walls and there are cracks in the wall. Like the quake in Mexico City: I am on the bed with Billy beside me and I notice the light shade on a cord from the ceiling is shaking and I think one more quake and I'd better take Billy out to the Sears Roebuck parking lot half a block away.

I didn't remember the quake dream until I saw the newspaper lead on the quake in San Salvador on Friday, October 10, 1986.

Loud talk with Brion about who is and who is not native to this planet. We are talking over coffee in a cafe. I glance up from the table and see a very pale young man drinking from a glass. He's got a dead look and I realize he is a dummy in some arrangement. A Hopper perhaps. And I formulate one clear sentence about this matter of natives: "He is native to the place if the place can't exist without him."

A place to fish at the end of a cobblestone street. Deep blue water. Someone has thrown in a float and it is already bobbing.

Portland Place. Empty house. Leaves blowing, drifting like shreds of time. Radio silence on Portland Place. Furtive seedy figures, rooming houses and chili parlors, hop joints, cathouses.

Fresh southerly winds. New York. A remote curtained drawing room. Marble mantelpiece. Decanter of port. A table. Maps and blueprints.

"There are many alternatives."

I am riding in a subway, in the lead car. The motorman is just in front of me, but concealed by a blind half drawn down. There are only a few other passengers in the car and then there are none. End of the line. The car is quite small now, with metal walls of dull gray but not painted, and I begin to feel suffocated. The train is not moving. I pound on the walls.

Next night. I have come to the end of the subway line. The area is circular. There are two other people there. They are sitting in a sunken circle in the middle of the station. I tell them the train is not going any farther and I am getting off here.

I walk up some steps into a station. High ceiling . . . a large arched entrance leading to the street. I think, This is St. Louis, and now Mort comes to greet me. He is young and handsome, wearing a black Chesterfield, a white shirt, and a tie of red and black pattern. He will introduce me to family relatives I have never seen before, who are sitting on benches waiting to meet me. At the end of the bench is a man with a very large face and a black suit who glares at me and I don't know why he is not included in the reception line of relatives. So I smile at him in case he is a relative, but he does not smile back. Now these relatives are standing up and form a reception line and I start greeting them one after the other.

Nowhere. I am in someone else's apartment. What am I doing here? Could be considered burglary, though I am not stealing anything. A messy, anonymous, confused apartment from anywhere. Out a window onto a narrow ledge. At the end of the ledge is a ladder of broken rotted wood, painted white, which does not reach all the way to the ground about twenty feet down. Bushes and trees down there and I hear people talking about "Mr. Burroughs . . ." and I know they are planning to kill me.

Subways, train stations, airports, boats . . . travel, all the time clutching my hotel keys, the only connection I have. The only home I have. I constantly reassure myself by feeling the key there in my pocket. Not that it means very much, since there is no privacy in the area.

Back in 77 Franklin. A stairway leading up to my old apartment, which was different and occupied by someone else. There was a kitten there.

Talking to Paul Getty III and my father in Italy. We are in a parked car by something that looks like Central Park. I am talking in a sophisticated, knowing way about drugs and such, and wonder if Dad will be upset, but it's time he learned about the birds and the bees, I guess.

We walk into a dead-end street that ends in a large circular court which is also a cafe and there is a passage to the left side that is both a cafe and a right-of-way to the streets beyond. A waitress immediately says: "What do you want?"

We ignore her and walk on through. There was more foolery yet.

The usual mixture of rooms and squares and streets that is the mark of the Land of the Dead. Streets lead into kitchens and bedrooms, so no area is completely private or completely public.

Like in the *New Yorker* cartoon of people trooping through a barbershop. Barber at the phone: "Is this the IRT? I'd like to report a leak . . ."

There were two of us sentenced to be hanged in some foreign country. (Obvious reference to the two Australians hanged in Malaysia. When small-time drug trafficking is equated with murder all sense of proportion has been lost.) We have armed ourselves, and we come to a wall with a gate and lock. I see now a six-foot snarling rabbit, and there are others outside the wall . . .

The dream I am about to relate illustrates the inadequacy of words when there are simply no equivalent meanings. To begin with, it is not a dream in the usual sense, being totally alien to any waking experience. A vision? No, not that either. A visit is the closest I can come. I was there. If I could draw or paint with accuracy, or better still, if I had a camera . . .

Walking down a passageway. The whole area seems to be enclosed—by inference, that is: I never see the sky or anything beyond. I look up and see a handsome boy of about nineteen on a balcony with an older youth about twenty-three or so. The balcony is about thirty feet above the passageway, and the building is red brick. Someway, I get up on the balcony. Behind is a small room with several other people.

The boy is wearing a white shirt with a yellow tie. Now the older youth takes a crossbow, though instead of the bow sticking out on both sides, it is set vertically on the shaft. He puts the bow between the boy's legs—there is an arrow in the bow (double-edge hunting arrow, three inches long and two inches at the base) pointed up to the boy's groin—and pulls the trigger. For some reason the arrow does not hit the boy. I gather this is some sort of test and I am next. I stand without flinching. The bowman says I have passed the test and that now I am one of them. We shake hands.

There is one there who has not passed the test. He is more like a doll than a person, with what appears to be a detachable head. Next, we form a line, one behind the other, and they are showing me how our muscles can become attuned so we are one body. There is a further lesson which I do not understand, involving balance or movement. I want to explore further but want to return later. So I make a note of the spot.

I look down the passageway, which is somewhat like an airport, and walk down. At the end to my right, I come to a square about sixty feet on each side. White stone buildings around the three sides but no windows or doors. Just a few slots or round openings.

Someway this square was connected with the Christian religion. I can see nobody but I feel that there are eyes watching me. Around the walls of the square are what appear to be glass ornaments of some kind, but I can't be sure they are made of glass, nor do I have any clear idea as to what they look like.

I leave the square to the left and there is an area like a living room or a waiting room with potted plants and two people sitting on a couch, one of whom looks vaguely like Jacques Stern, and I ask if his name is Stern. Others gather around: one has a strange, large, white face and a smile that seems painted on. He is formal with me and wishes to introduce himself, but I don't catch the name. I think I should get back to the place where I made a connection and was received.

But I look, now, down a side street and some distance away is a very high building . . . perhaps seven hundred to a thousand feet high, surrounded by other buildings in some red stone. It looks very alien and magnificent and I want to see the large buildings from inside. The roof is shaped like an arch . . . like a huge Quonset hut.

I come to a door in yellow oak which I push open . . . down a large hallway into a large room. But this is not the inside of the large building. Not nearly high enough. But still quite large. There are a number of people there, moving around, engaged in incomprehensible pursuits. I am attacked viciously by a small dog which is biting my hand. It *hurts*. I manage to transfer the dog's jaws to another small dog, wirehaired and black.

I am sitting by a round cage . . . like a zoo aviary. In the cage there are a number of people dressed in some ceremonial costumes. They are, I gather, a presidium. Sitting next to me on a high stool or chair is a tiny boy, not more than a foot high, but thick and with a large head. His face is perfectly smooth, like ceramic. A very handsome and perfect face. He does not move or speak. I walk away, towards a door, still trying to find the inside of the large building. Turning, I see a boy four feet tall with an inhumanly beautiful face and a buckskin jacket . . . like a figure in my painting "The Magic Rose Garden."

I've seen him with just a glance over my shoulder. Did he notice? I don't think so. In fact no one in this area has acknowledged my presence. Except the dog. The miniature boy or man sitting beside me could have been a ceramic statue. No movement, not even blinking.

I open a door, which leads to a square, boxlike room about fifty feet on each side by forty feet high. The walls and floor are white, but unlike Christian Square, this looks like white polished wood and the room is definitely closed at the top, unlike the stone square, which is open on top . . . though I could not see the sky. This wooden room reminds me of a surrealist painting of birdhouses and running figures in the distance. There is a humming sound and the room communicates a strident menace. As if something could pop out of the walls on springs or the room could suddenly shrink down to a birdhouse.

I wake up but it is more like a return. In this experience I have no feeling of dreaming. It is completely real. I am there. It is also definitely alien and unpleasantly so. I have no feeling of being in control, especially not in the two white squares. Both communicate potential danger—incalculable danger. Note that there is no line between streets and private house—all doors seem to be open. This line is a convention of Planet Earth and does not apply in these areas.

Private rooms? Streets? What do these distinctions mean?

Don't play anymore, but they understood sometimes an animal sick in Daddy the noises go thin dies and Fluffy with wave the sound good my mind's been listening you down to drown. I'm going to call the police. They even brought in boy's body. He'll kill the ocean, thank you. Must need that money. Think of the fair. I really grasped. Expect you will. A soft slow rain wetting just doesn't fit in with life and she was wailing, a thin-looking kind of a wail. Left hand and wrist right off in my eyes. These were his words. We'll meet again. Don't mistake snatch in my direction.

Blue used to be my favorite color. Since I have started to paint, it has shown itself as the most difficult color to work with. Blue is unmagical. It is just *blue;* there are no nuances, no extensions. Rarely do figures and faces appear in a blue painting. Just blue on paper and that is all. Very occasionally I get lucky with blue. The association of blue with money. Blue-chip stocks. Cool remote blue boardrooms. And with junk. Cool blue mineral calm. Perhaps blue is a *quantitative* color.

A blue picture I have just completed. I look for some meaning, some life. There is none. The blue paint even clogs the drain in the sink.

I can hear voices outside the door to the bedroom, which is closed. Like speeded-up voices on a tape recorder. I open the door with my "Snubbie" in my hand. Four or five children are there with their faces painted, in Halloween trick-or-treat costumes. Now I can hear them yacking in other rooms. Light in the front room won't turn on. Waking up. Bill, James, and Brion there. I am relating the dream.

"I heard voices outside the door. Think it is just an illusion, but when I open the door there are these children." At this point, one of the children is going down the basement steps and I point to him and say to James: "Look there. Real enough, isn't he?"

Brion is going to a sweat lodge. He is wearing an undershirt and jeans.

I go into the bathroom. A boy is sitting on the toilet seat, which is now on the other side of the bathroom where the towel rack is. He does not appear to be defecating. He says: "I don't want to go back to Smith."

These children are about ten years old.

With Carl Weissner in Germany. I ask him: "Just where are we? Germany? Belgium?" There is a gray beach . . . fog-gray water. The beach is about fifteen feet below street level. Rotten pilings. I go down to the beach, which is coarse gray gravel.

Brion and I in Germany. Fused together somehow at the sides. Our cheeks together. Reincarnation of Hitler?

My room is open and some agents are searching the rooms.

I say: *"Was machen Sie hier?"*

First time I ever spoke German in a dream?

Taking a shower in a small town in Germany. Talking about Tony Dutch. People laugh at everything I say. "Tony Dutch gets a habit every two months and never gets over the last habit before he starts again."

I am writing a film script for Dutch Schultz.

I am in England talking to a red-haired boy, with a dead white face, and his companion, someone I cannot see clearly. They are going to France. I am in London and tempted to go with them. After all, there is nothing but a blue suitcase in my hotel room. However, I turn back, with the boy's strange white face clearly imprinted in my mind.

Junk-sick in Tangier. I am going to show James "the most horrible street in Tangier." Reference to the ghetto street. We are walking down a street towards what looks like a dead end. However, there is a narrow opening at the end to the left which brings us into a corridor. Not the street I am looking for.

I turn into a room at one end of the corridor and see that I have entered someone's house. There is a young man there with reddish hair, wearing a brown suit and pants. His face, if it could be so called, is a pale white color with red markings. There seems to be neither mouth, nose, nor eyes. Just a place where the face would be . . . the outlines. I apologize. He says nothing.

Turn back to the corridor, which is lined with pinball machines on the far side. None of them are in use and, in fact, no one is visible. It's as if there is only enough light to illuminate a small area . . . a little patch of light surrounded by darkness. I had this feeling during my last visit to Tangier.

The city has shrunk down to the Minzah Hotel. The only light left is there. The feeling of a model, like a dollhouse, not that the actual rooms and furniture are small, measured by someone within the lighted area, but small in comparison with the surrounding blackness.

I am looking for a place to shave. I live in a cubicle room with my three cats and there is a rusty basin with a cold-water tap. I decide to shave at Allen Ginsberg's, which is just up the street. A maze of streets, rooms, corridors, cul-de-sacs, doorways so narrow one must squeeze through sideways, huge open courtyards and rooms. I decide to take two cats to Allen's place, which consists of a bathtub in a small room. I can shave using the bathtub. Look around to find that my cats are gone. I reach under the bathtub and pull out a long, thin, gray cat but can't find my cats. Is there an opening? I should have left them at home.

I come into a huge roofless room where there are statues and altars, all on a very large scale. Outside is a courtyard surrounded by wooden buildings. Character of buildings shifts and changes here. A French influence. Produces a sloping narrow street of vaguely Parisian cast. I see a doorway etched in blue and purple.

The number is 62. A cul-de-sac stone cell. A cabinet from which a strange club pops out, up through a hole in the top. I try to grab the club, but it is uncontrollable. Animated by shift of weight. It is about two feet long, covered in garish Aztec mosaics in purple and orange and purple and pink, like some hideous skin disease.

I turn to a small open showcase which contains a small hammer in some shiny metal like stainless steel. There are other objects of the same metal, which I cannot remember, since they could not be classified as serving any recognizable function. I simply did not have a place in my mind to store such data. I try to pick up the hammer, which is about six inches overall, but it is heavy to lift and, like the club, subject to sudden shifts of weight, so that if I get the handle partway up, the weight suddenly moves from the head to the handle. There is something very unpleasant about the heaviness of the hammer and the way it keeps jumping or sliding out of my hand.

Now a man is standing there, but I can see only his head and shoulders, which are very large. His face is pale. He has a mustache and very clear gray eyes. He looks like a soldier in the Civil War. He says something that I cannot understand.

A boy in a swimming pool . . . Turkish bath. We make it, then I look out at a vista of railroads and afternoon sunlight stretching into the distance. Can I step right out into this region, keep going and never come back?

Talking to Michael Portman and Ted Morgan. Ted is much younger, and slim. We are talking in a cafeteria. President Eisenhower, also slimmer and younger, shows me the entrance to a building.

I have to pack and there is very little time.

Very strange nightmare last night. There is a boy in my bed. About fifteen, dark with a round face, quite good-looking, dark eyes. He is holding in his hand a metal tube about three and one half inches long and half to three quarters of an inch in diameter, like a cigarette lighter. At the end of the tube is a short flame like a miniature blowtorch, and the boy keeps saying "Mason!" or "Machen!" which is apparently the name of this instrument, which is, I know, somehow deadly dangerous, and he is threatening to apply this "Mason" to me, which would be fatal. However, there is no trace of threat in the round young face. He seems to be naked except for a garment like a karate jacket.

"Mason! Mason! Mason!" he says over and over, as the tube flares up.

Then as I wake up, the boy fades and behind him is the spectral figure of Paul Bowles, fully dressed, with a coat and tie . . . transparent . . . I can see the wall behind him.

Fully awake now, I can feel a shiver up the back of my neck. What could "Mason" mean? Well, there is Mason Hoffenberg . . . (Oven Town) . . . which reminds me of my oven ordeals. But the boy is nothing like Mason. Not at all Semitic-looking . . . rather, Arab or Latin.

Back to sleep and the dream continues, but without the paralyzing fear of the first episode. I see Billy, very small, but walking like an adult, with suppurating pustules all over his back. Dad is there, and we take Billy to another room.

Now I am standing up in a strange dark room and raise my arms and look in a mirror, but before my image is clear I fall through the mirror and down some stairs into a sort of storeroom.

There is some attack mounted for three o'clock. I am looking for my .45. My guns are in a cabinet behind the bed, but there is no lock. I am not sure who will attack us or who, exactly, "we" are.

Wake up again.

Sores on Billy's back? I remember when I was living with Jack Anderson on West Twelfth Street, NYC. He had a nightmare and was up and walking away from someone who had sores all up and down his back that he was trying to show to Jack. Now who could that have been?

Back to sleep.

It seems that Dr. Eissler, my old psychoanalyst from Chicago, was giving a talk. I am reluctant to go all the way out there by subway. Couldn't I just skip it? For some reason I must attend.

Wake up again.

Last episode: I am in an apartment. There are, perhaps, five rooms opening off a corridor. The whole structure is cheaply built. There is someone at the door who looks like an old picture of myself from some dust jacket. But it is somehow Ian. I ask him to come in, but he says: "I just wanted to give you this," and hands me a copy of the Paris *International Herald Tribune.* I take the paper and walk along the corridor to the master bedroom where the gun cabinet is.

As regards "Mason," I find that something so completely inexplicable usually refers to some future intersection point.

Big air crash last night at the Kansas City airport.

Strange notation on the paper beside my bed on a chair.

"Power Faiture. I mean Power Failure 13."

No memory of this. I read an article on power failure in *Smith-sonian* magazine—that is, I skimmed through it. Power failure . . . hmmmm . . . fate or the French *fait,* fact, as in *fait accompli.* Translate as Power Fate Your . . . or Power Fate You Are.

Billy was in bed, sick, in a bare room with a river outside. There is no wall to the room on the side facing the river. I had observed two Phoenicians standing on the ice floes. It looks very precarious, I suppose they are swept out to sea? Well, at least they have oars and are quite close to shore.

Billy is in a large bed with a brown blanket. Dr. John Dent is the attending physician. I feel that Dr. Dent is not taking as serious a view of the case as the symptoms warrant. I suggest that Billy has a skin condition. The previous day I had read an article on Paul Klee, who suffered from some skin disease called scleroderma which turned his skin into a kind of armor.

I leave the room and walk down a short corridor into another room. A small room with a low arched ceiling of oval shape, the ceiling arching downward so that it touched the floor at the ends of the room, and there were also little niches in the wall. The whole room was in white plaster, like a tomb, and I began to fear that the door would close and seal behind me. A recurrent nightmare in which I go down stairs that get narrower and narrower and then a door closes behind me. Sometimes the cul-de-sac is a room rather than stairs. I have learned to avoid these traps in my dreams. So now I hastily step back through the door and down the corridor.

Meanwhile the house has become a ship. I have a ticket and I enter the room where Billy was, which is now carpeted in red, with my baggage. Someone tells me to get off the stage. This is a film, and I can feel the boat moving as I step back into the wings.

The boat stops. There is no boat. Just the empty house and the white plaster walls. I walk down the corridor and through the rooms. Nobody has been here for a long time. I am overwhelmed by desolation and sadness, and wake up groaning.

Ian . . . sort of made it. He catches a thought like a ball.

I repeated, "I will remember my dreams."

On a quay I saw blue goats and black goats. It was in Tangier or Egypt. There were canals between rivers. John Cooke was there.

Animals outside through a wire mesh door, a huge pig with piglets suckling. A number of dogs, one of which was mine, and cats in a sex orgy.

Gregory was there and we are going to split some heroin.

The house at Price Road. A walking corpse. Many cats. Another mother came into the room. She had rather short blond hair and looked nothing like Laura. Her face was reminiscent of Lucien Carr in his youth.

In Bogotá with Brion. He steered me to a junk drop in the basement of a tobacconist, where I got a shot.

Crowds of people milling about in city square.

Three miniature soldiers about three feet high, with black mustaches and guns. Look Japanese.

In a train . . . faster and faster. I think we will surely crash. Going to reach Frisco, but we'll all be dead. George Kaull is at the throttle, I think.

Faster and faster . . . ninety miles an hour.

Walking in a strange city. I was composing a short story called "The End of the Line." This seemed to be in eastern Siberia, just across the Bering Strait. I arrive with one suitcase and a bottle of morphine pills . . . dying of cancer.

English police in my apartment. James is in there and the location was not here. I was talking to an English cop, very high up, who knew I was not guilty of whatever I was charged with. He had a dark clean-shaven face. Obviously he is the Assistant Commissioner in Conrad's *Secret Agent*.

I was home in 4664 Pershing Avenue, but reversed order of rooms. I am on the second floor at the rear of the house. Very run-down and dirty. The lights do not work. Then a ghostly intruder appears in the open doorway which led to a hall and another room. He is wearing a white robe of some kind, with yellow markings. I am so paralyzed with fear that I cannot pull out my snub-nosed .38.

Across the hall in another room I see Brion propped up in bed. Alan Watson is with him and asks me for some heroin. I have a very small amount, mixed with hash.

Jacques Stern is in Morocco. There is a drugstore at the end of a corridor. Jacques slips in behind the counter and refuses to fill an Rx for chloral hydrate. I am left in a dreary empty hall with murky darkness outside.

Then take a walk with J.S. A street like a corridor. Come to another street, very narrow, steeply slanting upward into a putrid light with the hermetic ghetto. Smell of thousands of years of unwashed clothes and people in shuttered rooms.

Fletch just jumped up on the table and I pet him behind the ears and over his strong muscled back and realize *what a male* creature he is. Little Calico is a delightful female beast like Jane Bowles and Joan and Mother . . . a little spirit romping around. When I pick her up she makes a weak cry of protest. She has never scratched at me, which is extraordinary. I still have claw marks from Fletch. They go deep and heal slow. Sometimes she *almost* scratches me, like this afternoon when she whined outside my closet and then jumped up on some shirts and socks and underwear and I reach in and she almost scratches me, then pulls herself back. I wouldn't hurt her. I wouldn't slap her. She has never been mistreated in her life, and I was present at her birth. She has never been slapped.

Since a number of dreams are set in the house at Price Road, 700 South Price Road, I will indicate how that house was, and probably still is, laid out: Ground floor, front door opens into hall. To the left of door, dining room. Behind dining room is kitchen and servant quarters and back door. To the right is living room. Upstairs a back room with two beds, two closets, and a window on three sides, where Mort and I lived and slept. Bathroom and guest room. Above living room is room where Dad and Mother slept. Bathroom. Balcony opening onto garden.

Last night, dream David Budd is with me in back room. Since he often signs his letters "Brother Budd," association is obvious. In dream there is only one large bed. I suggest he use bed in parental bedroom, and we go there. Coming from bathroom is radio broadcast. I think it is a newscast. David Budd is telling me about an island off the coast of Florida. Name is something like Sploetti. He says very nasty people live there.

I find myself there in the capacity of a hospital administrator. Forty beds, two occupied by women patients. I ask if they would like a shot of morphine. They say they would. Looking for narco cabinet. An orderly shows me that you press a button and it opens. Vials with screw tops. Can't assemble injections. Any case, nobody challenges my incumbency.

Looking back through old dream notes I find:

With David Budd in East St. Louis. Tunnels under drugstore. Old hotel. Five little dogs. I suspect them to be door dogs, small dogs who bring death or misfortune when they follow someone across a threshold. East St. Louis is a run-down place with strata from the 1920s and back to the riverboat days. Rural slums . . . corn growing in backyards. Sidewalks with weeds growing through cracked pavement. On one side a fifteen-foot drop with limestone and jagged masonry outcropping to vacant lot. Weeds, brambles, broken masonry and bricks. Whorehouses and gambling joints. Still a heroin drop, I understand.

In the room at Price Road. I find there is someone in bed with me. First I think, Can it be my cat Ruski, but much too big. It's a man! I keep saying "Mort! Mort!" Can it be Mort, who slept in the bed across the room? But it isn't. I see his face finally, an ugly wooden face. It is dark in the room, but looking to the east I see it is daylight outside . . . blue sky and sunlight. I am trying to get the blinds up to let the light in.

The razor inside the filing cabinet. Categories that delineate a name. Biological revolution and see San Francisco dispersed. AIDS loss of outline loud and clear. Death bones of cold cigarette butts. Its secret name is Handle. Cut the lines. Nothing is my name. Like it? I declare biologic homeless despair. A picture city. Grain elevator just so. Where is a snapshot is my name. My purpose can see the room. Risk it!

So I jolt to an end in my Model T which boils. End of the line. Nothing more to say. Here we are. Look around at the 1920s, the 1930s. Look around. Nothing here. Look at Bradshaw, Texas, a ghost town. Dust and emptiness. The quick-draw is dead. The Old West is dead. Quick *and* dead.

A writer's will is the winds of dead calm in the Western Lands. Point way out he can start stirring of the sail. Writer, where are you going? To write. Here we are in texts already written on the sky. Where he doesn't need to write anymore. A slight seismic with the cat book. Always remember, the work is the mainsail to reach the Western Lands. The texts sing. Everything is grass and bushes, a desert or a maze of texts. Here you are . . . never use the same door twice. Sky in all directions . . . on the word for word. The word for word is word. The western sail stirs candles on 1920 country club table. Each page is a door to everything is permitted. The fragile lifeboat between this and that. Your words are the sails.

Ian and I are in a hospital. He wouldn't, as usual. A large oil painting, brown balloon-shaped figurations crossed with grid in black. Like old hot-air balloons. There are many entries to the Western Lands. The mark is a feeling of serene joy. It may be a flash of sunlight on muddy water. A house. A particular house . . . the porch made of large yellow stones in a matrix. Iced tea . . . calm peace . . . another house in North St. Louis . . . on a hillside . . . a garage . . . bits of vivid and vanishing detail. An apartment house . . . outskirts of Chicago. Nice Japanese. A sea whiff on the wind was its music. A moving camera. A run-down patio. Bougain-villea. Purple flowers underfoot . . . Tangier . . . Marrakech . . . Palm Beach, L.A. Tornado watch. Go out rather than take refuge in the flooded basement. Are the pumps holding their own? Re-member sea story. Turn on the pumps. We're shipping water and our muscles bulge to tremendous size. Wish I could get down there and pump it out.

I have been suffering from paralyzing depressions. Sometimes I se-riously ask myself how anyone can feel this bad and live. Often I simply collapse in ed. I mean bed, of course . . . come to think of it, never had a lover named Ed.

This is not some superattenuated, arcane, exclusive depression known only to the chosen and distinguished few. It is a realization of the raw horror of the human position at this point. Most people, of course, say: "Well, things past remedy should be past thought," and go about their stupid everyday concerns. Now what gives rise to the most dead hopeless depression? Withdrawal from opiates. I have noticed further that the depressions alternate with excesses of emotion; with emotional excesses, with tears and grief, also a symp-tom of withdrawal.

There are no innocent bystanders. What were they doing there in the first place? Like the woman who was hit and killed by a fragment from the helicopter that fell over on its side on top of the Pan Am building. Friends are urging me to use this helicopter, but I had a bad feeling about it. Hell of a location. Suppose it crashes right onto the evening rush at Grand Central Station? And I quote: "Be not the first by whom the new is tried, nor yet the last to lay the old aside." And sure as shit and taxes this accident happens a week later. The copter has landed and then falls onto its side and kills a nineteen-year-old youth on his way back somewhere. And a woman walking along Madison Avenue was hit and killed by a piece of the propeller.

Rilke said: "Give every man his own death." This seems as far as possible from any tailor-made death. She is walking down or up Madison Avenue, after eating in a cafeteria, before eating or shopping. Works there, doesn't work there, way out of orbit there, and suddenly two pounds of metal hits her in the back of the head. What were her last thoughts? The last words in her mind? No one will ever know.

And on my birthday, years ago in New York, someone suggested we go to the Blue Angel nightclub. I remember my first wife, Ilse, said about the proprietor: "He is such a piece of slime." Any case, I had a bad feeling about the Blue Angel, so we didn't go. It was about ten days later, there was a fire in the Blue Angel and something like twenty-three casualties.

Down a corridor. Much like the corridor at La Guardia Airport that leads past the newsstand to the restaurant. In a room where there was a Russian dinner all ready under a serving cover. With vodka, caviar, and all the trimmings. There is also a whore named Vicki in the room.

"Compliments of your friendly KGB."

Vicki is a proper horror, shaped like a pyramid, tapering to narrow shoulders. Set on a solid base of huge buttocks. I don't think I can make it, and want to start in on the Russian dinner instead.

In the house at Price Road tried to lumber a boy past Mother. No go. There are bits of metal in my lungs. Mother says I am the typical agent.

Sharing a room with Allerton. He is sulky and I say: "If you don't show some consideration, you can get out of here."

This shakes him. We are on the point of making it.

Number 9 rue Git le Coeur closed by the French police. Antony and Brion brutally arrested and taken away. I ran out around a porch and then into a cleft in a rock, looking for an underground station. There was no pursuit.

Walking on water. A river or canal that was at once clear and dirty. I could see to the bottom. The water was ten feet deep or more . . . streaks of dirt like black gauze floated under the surface.

I found Ruski . . . but his hair was all white except for his head. He had come from the Hotel Chelsea and I wasn't sure I could find the way to carry him back there. Besides, it is a long way to go.

In South Africa a person was showing me around in his car. He is rather chunky, with a mustache and a bodyguard. The car is long and white. He parks it, all illegal, in front of a bar which is on a number of levels, with a river running alongside it. I go in the bar, which is a semicircle, and find my way blocked by two boys about fifteen in dark suits who stand in front of me and go through a series of shadowboxing rituals. Not actually hitting me but, like I say, some sort of strange ritual. I look for my protector, who was standing at the bar.

Down several levels . . . this is the underworld of South Africa, though I can't see any blacks about. Bars under bars, each more sleazy and dangerous-looking than the one above. And here is a door off a corridor. I open the door and see that this is a steam room, very narrow and not more than fifteen feet long. There are wooden cubicles open in front and at the top, along the left side. A terrible smell of stale sweat and steamed excrement, like the room hasn't been cleaned in years. It is lit by a single yellow light bulb hanging down from the domed ceiling, which is dripping with condensed vapor that concentrates the horrible stink.

On a wooden shelf about four feet off the floor, a man is laid out. He looks like he is made from excrement, fired and glazed, with cracks at the shoulder and elbows, a dark brownish color with a slight glassiness to it, the face smooth, the eyes a pus-yellow color. Is it alive?

Back in the top bar, my protector says something or rather makes an admonitory gesture, and the two boys run and jump out through an open window like cats. One, in fact, turns into a cat as his body clears the sill.

Last night was Wayne Propst's fortieth birthday. I went to the party and gave him a sword cane. Some nutty woman of uncertain extraction . . . Negro, Indian, Japanese? She said that a captain had told her he had never had an accident. And what do you know . . . he had one the next day. Intense lady. Captain of what? A shithouse? When did this occur? In the 1970s? Sorry, I don't remember any captain.

Home early . . . to sleep, perchance to dream.

A party. I am home in bed and someone comes in. I can see through him. My hands are shaking so I can't hold the gun steady. Then he gets in bed with me. He looks something like Wayne. No longer frightened. Who or what is it? Wake up. Go back to sleep.

There he is again coming through a curtain in front of the doorway. He gets in bed with me. The encounter is vaguely sexual. He is half material, like I can see through him, but he is tactile and leaves a faint imprint on the bedclothes. He is wearing a gray suit that fades off him. As he comes in, Ginger jumps off the bed and runs out the door. I recognize him as a Project, a half-formed creature created from my thought forms. By now I feel very friendly towards him. (He is a Tulpa.)

Wake up. Make notes. Back to sleep. I am with Brion in a lecture hall looking for the notes to my lecture. They are in a black notebook with rings, the type of notebook I never use. I have given half of the lecture but the best part, which relates to AIDS, is in this notebook. At first I look around in a melodramatic manner. Then I realize I actually can't find the notebook. This disturbs me, because it is an excellent presentation, tracing the connection between Kaposi's sarcoma and AIDS.

In Paris with Mother and Dad. I wanted to see a museum of Madagascar. Took a train from Grand Central, careful to note the stops so I could find my way back. Had to change trains at right angles. Passed a palace. Very ornate building with barred windows and elaborate brickwork. But this is not the museum.

Then I get off the train and meet a man I know. He is French . . . small, thin, about fifty-five or sixty. He has a very small toothbrush mustache with a dividing line down the cleft. The mustache is black and his eyes are brown. His face is also a nut-brown color. I ask him about the museum and he is about to go into what looks like a classroom.

I can see an officer in uniform sitting in the front row. The man has a number on his lapel, number 7, I believe. He says: "Sorry. We are working," and goes back into the classroom. There is a short entrance hall and a coat closet. I don't know how to get back, and now I can't ask him.

The de C. family is in town. John is with his new wife and James tells me he has become very proper. It is a seaside place. I can see the gray water and the waves. I decide it is much too cold to go swimming. Now I am on the beach with François and the beach here is rather dirty. There is a pier to my left and seaweed and dead fish and driftwood on the beach.

Who is the little Frenchman? I know him from somewhere and I would know him again if I ever saw him. He could have given me very precise directions as to how to get back to Grand Central, but he is busy and I am not involved in whatever it is he is doing.

With Brion in a hallway. The lecture will continue at the clinic. It seems rather small. Just a single door in a rectangular building, adjacent to the hallway. He notices a building with flats to let. There are little windows in a wall. The open windows indicate the vacant flats. He goes in and calls up: "What floor are you on?"

There is a ladder that is pulled down like a fire escape ladder. He goes up one flight and finds the tenant in a bunk. The flat is behind him. A square room with red carpeting and a kitchenette in one corner. He is the proprietor, a thin middle-aged queen in a rubber suit like surfers use. He is in a hurry. He doesn't want to miss Brion, who is waiting in the hall. As he goes down the ladder, he calls back up: "Is there a bath, or just a shower?"

Reply is muffled. Outside, he finds Brion in the hall walking towards him.

Count Korzybski, no older than when I knew him in Chicago in 1938 and took his seminar. Face smooth, the strong heavy forearms. I have to take the *Bremen* for NYC.

Children by my bed who turn into rats that bite me. Big rats of an orange color with longish hair.

On some sort of stilts. The stilts now turn into an animal and I am crying and petting it and saying over and over:

"I'm sorry! I'm so sorry!"

In a room, a set, two women . . . one who appeared on a screen dying of cancer. She is about fifty-five, earrings, blue dress, distinguished in color. A fat man I quarrel with. Hit him in face and stomach. There is no force in my blows. He laughs. The women intervene on my behalf. I am ready to leave but can't find my cane.

Brion and someone else and myself coming up a stairway. Brion is trying to hold Ginger, who bites and scratches. She has run under a deserted building. I go in and she comes to me. She is very small . . . about the size of a ferret. I pick her up and carry her out.

Return I will to old Brazil. In Río. I am booked into the Chaguen Hotel. I meet Kells Elvins. The hotel is surrounded by corridors rather than streets. Smooth red tile floors with turnstiles and shops and restaurants, all closed in, like one vast structure. This is, of course, usual in the Land of the Dead.

In the lobby I am talking to the manager. He is, I think, Italian, wearing a gray suit with a black mustache . . . in his mid-thirties. He wants to get out of Río and go to Rome where he will drive his ──────── (name of a car not clear or referring to no make known to me).

In a theater like a school gymnasium, all the seats on the same level. I am trying to start a fire. There are some papers under Kells' seat and I am trying to light them . . . knowing that he will have ample time to get out. He can, in fact, see what I am doing. But the matches won't light . . . three matches go out. One more try.

In doorway like Lawrence Community Center, where the pistol range is located. Two boys point to a round mark or logo on my shoes. These are not the shoes I ordinarily wear. They are high shoes in brown suede. Like the high suede shoes I had made in London that never quite fit me and are now in the Bunker. The mark was like a little tattoo at the ankle. In blue and red I think, like the tattoos that youth gangs in the Philippines use to identify their particular band.

Picture in one of the scrapbooks shows boys with their pants down and a cop is pointing to a tattoo on the side of a boy's buttock: "Ahhhhaa. Look at that!"

The boys are slim and beautiful. Boys in the dream are American-looking, very much like the boy who plays Huckleberry Finn in a TV serial. About fifteen. They are blocking my way. Their intention and attitude ambiguous . . . not hostile, not friendly.

A Chinese cop hassled me about my Kiyoga, a spring blackjack. He had a badge pinned to his chest. In a theater of some sort. It was closing, but one could see the film through a little peephole, like a periscope head. Ian was watching the film, but I thought this was ridiculous. The theater was closed and I was looking for my cane and my coat. The manager, who was an old Jew, gave me a coat and I put it on, but it wasn't my coat at all. It was too short and the sleeves came up to my elbows.

The Monkey's Head. Brion was there and I pick up the monkey's head and prepare to make a wish. I felt it move, I tell you, like the bulkhead in *Lord Jim.* It will give way at any second and wishes will gush out and it will be . . . "*Sauve qui peut.*" Every man for himself! . . . when the wishes spurt out and they all have validity unless negated by counterwishes, which puts all the wishes into furious, deadly, and often suicidal competition.

Ian and Brion and a boy and myself sitting on a bench. The boy is very young, about seventeen, with a few pimples . . . quite attractive. I saw him today in the Town Crier. Ian is going off with the boy and I am very annoyed. I go to have dinner with Brion, or perhaps spaghetti by myself.

I rise out of my body and cross the room at ceiling height. My body is still on the bed and now I slip back into the body from the head down. Mikey Portman is pushing heroin. It is a strange blue color and I sniff some. His face seems to project at the mouth into a triangular shape, the teeth yellow and prominent. The skin around the mouth is smooth and yellowish.

Take an elevator to the top floor. It is one floor above where I live. I am looking for stairs to walk down. A sunrise or landscape. I say: "Perhaps it is poison gas."

I have to get my coat and cane to go to a class. I am back in school or university . . . swirling colors . . . "It may be poison gas." I don't really believe it.

A whole area with a patch of blue sky off to the left-hand corner outside the inside, which is a sort of gymnasium. I know that I am in the lower strata despite the patch of blue sky and that there is this area above where I am and above the sky itself or at least above my view of the sky. Now some people come down through a trapdoor and down ladders from the space above the upper level. They are neither young nor old, rather well dressed, but informal, all with tans. Three of them. They say nothing I can hear but they are talking. They are rather like the Ecotechnic Institute personnel.

A haunted room. I am attacked by a cat that turns into a ghost that bites. Then I see a small orange cat by my head on the pillow. I tell someone I will not sleep there again. Go up in an elevator to another apartment.

Otto Belue is talking about a battleship. I point out to him that it is simply a backhoe. He is projecting the concept of a battleship.

Jack Senseny at Mort's funeral. He never did anything . . . a little publicity work . . . Face heavily creased . . . emphysema I hear . . . terminal in any case.

And before Senseny there were three horrible centipedes, not very big. One of them seemed to have a smaller centipede of a bright red color inside it and this was the worst centipede of them all.

Stranded in the L.O.D. My room is $46 a night. Not sure I can stay another night. I am trying to phone to Paris and make a hotel reservation and then a boat or plane to America. But the phone is complex. I can't seem to get it to work. Ian has gone to Paris. I should have stayed with him. Where am I exactly? London? It is a hotel of some sort. Ira Jaffe shows up, but doesn't have any helpful suggestions. Feeling of being completely at a loss. How much money do I have? I take out my wallet to count it. There is something in the bed with me that moves. Wake up. It's the cat of course.

The $46 came from a TV show about welfare hotels. The reporter has taken a room in the Warren Hotel in Times Square. $46 per night.

A dreary complex subway station. Couldn't find the train.

Sitting at a table in despair. At the next table a man with very pale gray eyes said:

"Mr. Burroughs, why don't you call 6410?"

A sign, "Russell Hotel," over a door that leads from the station directly into the hotel. An iron stairway beside the sign leads to a narrow platform with tables for food and coffee.

Another of the breakfast or rather no-breakfast dreams, which now occur almost nightly and are no longer strictly confined to the Land of the Dead. I am in a hotel and the rooms are very large, forty feet or more across. Can I not simply pick up the phone, ask for room service, and *order* breakfast? I have tried this several times before, with negative results. Bill Rich tells me there is a grill downstairs where one can eat breakfast, and I proceed to another confusing elevator. To one side is a large open shaft. Colored murals on the other side . . . connected some way with Gibraltar.

Later I am in a room beside what appears to be a bus or perhaps a mobile home. There is a man there with a mustache and I ask him if he can do an imitation of Maurice Chevalier. He begins to sing a French music hall song . . . *"Ah oui oui Paris"* and dances himself up on top of the bus, where he is faced by two dogs, side by side, and four more dogs behind these. Eight in all. He dances towards the dogs, singing, his hands clasped behind his back, bent forward, his face extended towards the dogs, who now dance backward off the end of the bus. Then one dog comes around from behind the bus with a collar and short length of rope around its neck.

I am in Madrid and go to a place of many cats and dogs to adopt a kitten. It is a small black kitten. There are clouds of flies around and I take the kitten and a blanket to shut out the flies.

The breakfast dreams have only started in the last six years or so, since I became preoccupied with the Land of the Dead. The dreams refer not only to breakfast but to difficulty in obtaining any sort of food, except for strange outlandish sweet dishes that are eaten more with the eyes than with the mouth. At one time or another there have been a number of dreams about flies . . . usually biting flies.

I meet some Rolling Stones, Mick Jagger and others, when they get off a bus. Outskirts of an American city. There is a deadly plague that seems to drive people insane and violent. It is moving in from rural areas to the cities. One of the pop group says he is going back to pick up some friends and then will return.

I say: "If you return."

Scene is now in NYC. I am on the Lower East Side and it looks like business as usual. I know that the plague hasn't hit yet, but will hit at any moment. Now I am trying to find my way back to my apartment, where I have some guns stashed. There are several people with me including, I think, Mick Jagger. I say: "Stay together and walk fast." Even the pavements and subways are falling apart and I can look down a thousand feet into girders and rubble. The plague is everywhere now. People are raving and stripping off their clothes. Corpses everywhere, whether from the plague or violence I can't be sure. It is total Pandemonium.

When I get back to the apartment it is simply a mass of rubble. However, two guns and a few knives have been salvaged and are on a wooden shelf. One gun is clearly antique, single-barrel, single-shot, with a breech that unscrews. The other looks like a .22 single-shot, but there are no cartridges. One knife is a large folder, but dull and corroded as if it had been in a fire. The other, a small folder with wood handle. None of these weapons looks serviceable. Some of the group I am with have been hit by the plague, which causes violent diarrhea and fainting spells.

Someone named John with a face like a mask. I could see the flesh mask around the eyes. I poke a hole in the ground with a stick and there is water just under the surface. A slope, maybe a hundred yards down. This piece of land curled at the edges. Masked face with the eyes peeking out. Who is this John? The slope is covered with branches of some tree or bush like evergreen. John tries to slide down the slope on these branches. I tell him it won't work, which indeed it will not.

Opening of *The Black Rider* at the Thalia Theatre in Hamburg. A green lawn. Ian is talking to a woman in a white dress. Another woman behind a barricade pulls a toy gun.

A high school in South Africa. A man with a whip . . . another with a gun. Some beautiful blue-and-gold vases. They all learn apartheid here and all the rest of the South African program.

A quart of kerosene to be poured from one container into another. Second container is faulty, bottom loose. Bottom falls out, spilling kerosene across the floor. I try to clean up with a paper napkin. There is kerosene on my thumb and forefinger. I can see it quite clearly. I wipe it off, but the odor remains.

With Alan Watson.

"We are here to offer our sympathy."

Exactly to whom are we offering sympathy and why?

There is a swamp. Cats and dogs about. A writing project involving a story from a book. Many pictures to illustrate the book. But I wonder about the writer of the story. "Doesn't he have a copyright?"

The lavishly illustrated book contains five short stories. The story we have chosen is the longest, but considering the pictures, not very long. The word "mother" appears in the title, and there is a reference to *The Temple* by Stephen Spender. Long walk from one end of the swamp to another.

Is this the Slough of Despond from *Pilgrim's Progress?*

IV injection in bottom of foot. Blood in syringe, but a leak. Association callus, and need to call Dr. Gaston again for a treatment.

Rowing in Tangier Bay. Deep blue water. One of the oars is slipping down out of sight. Feeling of fear as the boat slowly gyrates out of control. Joan is there in a room, and I give her some fragments of opium.

Roast beef and mashed potatoes. "She died of poisonous puberty."

Painted piano rollers. With just the right twist and push, you can twist your opponent's gut out. I learned the art from Oozie the Twist.

A little twelve-year-old black boy with a toy gun says: "I want to be your friend."

Looking for breakfast in Paris, on the weed-grown bank of a river, deep blue water and boats. To my right, the river runs into a lake. Waves sparkling in the moonlight.

An intruder at the Price Road house.

The Pale Piper. A robe of pale yellow, a pipe of amber. Going to see Dr. Riock. Couldn't find my room as usual in the Land of the Dead. Followed by bounty hunters. What am I worth? Gregory wanted to borrow money. Ian there. I am waiting for Johnny Robbins. Arrive at customs with a pound of pot. Fine of $1,000. Female agents. Ian going up into an apartment. Later in a cafeteria Ian comes to my table with a sliced strawberry roll. Same roll eaten by Jerry in fairground area. We are going down into NYC and I say: "Broadway always wears a smile."

Usually the looking-for-breakfast dream is in the L.O.D., as I soon discern by looking around at the personnel. They are all dead. In this case, no. James arrives and we are going to have breakfast in the Kansas Union cafeteria. I see people lined up and maybe it's too late. Empty tables and chairs stacked upside down. There is one counter open where some sort of weird sandwiches are sliced off a bone. They are round in shape. The server is English and insolent.

I finally get my so-called sandwich wrapped in brown paper and it looks like part of a dismembered body—a cylinder of bone in the middle of some nameless meat. Looking around, I can't find James. Finally spot George Kaull. Looking for the others, I see a counter with soft drinks and ask for a cup of coffee and an insolent little bitch says: "We don't give out coffee. You have to bring it."

The dead around, like bird calls. Dr. Bronquist. Peter Lacy. Jay Hazelwood, who ran the Parade Bar. Fruity gondolier murals on the walls. A patio with trees and wobbly iron tables. Jay died in the Parade on Christmas day. He went to the WC and came out sweating and went into the kitchen, lay down on the kitchen floor and died and Randy, the unspeakable Randy Means, took advantage of the confusion to steal a thousand francs from Jane Beck's purse.

A lake. Boats to my right. Call Dr. Gaston from a moonlight bay. Deep blue water. One of the sights feeling of fear pipe of amber control. Joan is there in a room as usual in the Land of the Dead. In the Land of June 11, 1990. Roast beef hunters. What am I worth? "She died of poisonous puberty" there. I am waiting for painted piano rolls with just a pound of pot. Can twist your apartment from Oozie the Twist. A twelve-year-old black boy says: "I want to be your friend." Looking for breakfast in Paris. The Pale Piper slowly gyrates out to see Dr. Riock. Give her some fragments of the Dead followed by gravy and mashed potatoes. Ian and Jonathan Robbins arrive at the right twist and push you. Female agents Ian guts out I learned later in a cafeteria. Ian comes to my strawberry roll. With a toy gun says: "Broadway always wears a smile."

Vivid color dream. Seems that Kells has been busted on a narcotics charge and they are looking for me. (Call from Dean Ripa. Offers to pay my way to Costa Rica. Many flying saucer sightings.) Walking around in a city looking for a place to hide. An elaborate fountain with scrollwork in stone and an overhang, but not enough space to hide. Wading and finally swimming in water. I know they will have the clinic staked out and I am already sick. Empty streets. Wake up and back to sleep. Same script.

Now I am on a street in England. No methadone left. I go into a building with luxurious apartments. Pink blankets. Beds, fine furniture. Someone is coming in. There is an ornate tiled fireplace. Can I hide there? Too shallow. I have an old Colt pocket .32 APC. Two men come in. They see me right away. I threaten them with the gun. They just look at me, not at all impressed. One is tall with a smooth olive skin, dead black eyes, and a camel-hair overcoat. The other is short, wearing a white shirt. He is Oriental—Chinese or Japanese. They look like death squad personnel.

Someone has come into a room where I am.

"Mort! Mort!"

As a child I was afraid to be alone and was always relieved when Mort came home and I knew there was now somebody in the room with me. But this is not Mort. It is a stranger, rather fat, in a black overcoat, who moves with a strange gliding motion, not walking but sliding. I am paralyzed with fear, and can't get the top off a tear gas device.

Kiki has taken cough syrup with chloral hydrate. We go out to swim. A large lake or lagoon somewhat like the reservoir at Nederland, Colorado. Blue water reflects a red sun. I say it is too cold to swim—that is, the air is too cold. Kiki goes in the water and sinks out of sight. There is a deep spot a few feet from shore. He then surfaces. What he has stepped into is a huge shoe about six feet in length under the water. There is also various debris that would make swimming dangerous on this side of the lake.

In Madrid with Kiki. How can I get away without money? I will wire home but it will take several days. Want to make it with Kiki. I find a large four-poster bed with green sheets, rather dirty. Still, the bed will do. I hate Madrid and the thought of being stuck there. It was in Madrid that Kiki was stabbed to death by his jealous keeper who found him in bed with a girl. The jealous lover, who ran a band in which Kiki worked as a drummer, burst into the room with a butcher knife and killed Kiki. Then killed himself.

We are leaving for Denmark tomorrow, any chance of food? A bottle of Scotch. Message from Paul Bowles, 8:12 p.m. A buffet. I got an ice with red icing on top. Wanted the first dish. Couldn't find any. Saw some cookies. People there in and out—looking for food. Orgasm looking for food. Small place on several levels, looking for food. Empty plates.

We have taken over a small country. I want to be Chief of Police. Wouldn't you? Antony Balch very slim and young-looking. A perilous loft bed fifty feet up. Sex with James and Michael. People keep coming in. I order them out. They smile and simply go out one door, pop in another.

With Gregory in Rome. Get my key at the desk. They said I was on the second floor. Room 249. To my left a restaurant on two levels. People eating. Should I use the key? Not sure if it is the key for this room.

Passed Ian in a square room in Paris. He doesn't acknowledge. Brion says: "He doesn't see you."

Brion, Ian, and I in an apartment, Land of the Dead decor. Shabby, dusty. Brion tries to bring us together, but Ian objects and goes into a bathroom to take a bath. I follow him in. There are two other people here, but I say: "Listen, you son of a bitch, I've had enough . . ."

He says something like: "Justice. You must face me."

I walk out. Someone is guiding me through a series of doors and hallways. One door is a mottled brown-white color like one of my paintings. On and on. Come finally to a metal workshop. A man is moving a heavy steel drum. I ask:

"What the fuck do you do here?"

"Demolition."

"Can I work here?"

"You have to pass a physical."

He pointed out a dusty window across a courtyard littered with rubbish. I am feeling very free and happy and young. Across the yard is an outside wooden stairway, old and rickety, that leads to a landing which leads to a steep wooden stairway.

I go up the stairs into a loft. Two men are sitting in a corner. I ask if they are the doctors. One with mustache says: "Yes." He points across the loft. "What can you see?"

"A fifty-gallon drum. Some planks and paint cans and brushes and—"

"That's enough. Sight O.K." He points to a sledgehammer.

"Can you pick that up?"

I pick it up and heft it.

"All right. You can start tomorrow."

I go back to the shop. Looking out a window, I can see a long pier. Someone points.

"If you live over there, it's a long ways to work."

"Isn't there anyplace closer?"
"Yes, you can stay here."

I have been exposed to some radioactive device in Boston some
years ago. Now I am obliged to return to Taos, New Mexico, for a
follow-up. Someone called Cookie was also involved in the Boston
episode, but does not remember it.

In South Africa. Jesus has been hanged on a Thursday. I walk
through corridors and high-ceilinged empty rooms with parquet
floors, coming around in a semicircle to a clinic. It is a very large
old-fashioned building. I can see rows of bound paper and books.
I go in and introduce myself to an elderly gentleman in a gray suit
who says I can, of course, use the library, but it is too close to
closing time. Walk down a marble staircase, impressed by the old-
fashioned elegance and architecture. Finally jump about forty feet
down, landing by some women shoppers. No one pays any attention.
A religious cult leader harasses me, and I jump forty feet down into
a courtyard.

With James and Michael? In Paris way out at the end of the line
in a suburban area, *terrain vague*, of vacant lots and empty houses.
James picks up a flowerpot full of blue and white flowers and heads
for the subway, and I am afraid someone will come yelling after
him. Then I notice the house and yard look empty and abandoned.
I start to board the train, but I am too late. Way out in a district I
never saw before, and no idea how to get back and not at all sure
where I want to get back to.

Any case, I buy a ticket at a booth and start looking around for a map, when I meet this American and tell him I can't find a map and can't make out what maps I do see, and he says: "Yes, it's purely true," and I follow him down some stairs past colored posters or advertisements, down to a room like a tank. A square room about fifteen by fifteen with no windows. There are couch beds around the walls and several people there—men and women, all young and all American, and I get a whiff of coke.

Shift, and the room is empty except for one couch. The walls are a dirty white-orange color and there is a boy on the couch. He is naked to the waist, a smooth brownish torso. The mouth is thin and bloodless. He says something to the effect that "You will become me." I am not at all keen on the idea, and then he undresses all the way and he is uncircumcised, with a long wrinkled foreskin, doesn't even look like a phallus, and rank black hair growing between his legs down the thighs and up almost to the navel, and there are white spots in the skin under the hair, which is sort of greasy-looking. I float up to the ceiling and he says "Adios" in a resigned way. He didn't expect me to buy it.

A museum with a large wooden sculpture suspended by rope from the ceiling. Jack Kerouac was there, so looks like LOD. There was a shallow pond with yellow clay sides. One or two small fish. Beyond the pond was an office with desks and a work force of women. I go to the door of the office and tell them they have to leave. The business is on strike.

"What?" they say. "Leave our workplace?"

"Exactly," I say.

It seems that some woman named Pollyanna will come the following day at 7:00 p.m. to the Bunker kitchen, to "educate me in revolutionary theory and practice."

With Ian, cleaning out Dr. Dent's room. It is a small room, bare and dusty, with a single bed, crumpled sheets, and an Army blanket. I am using a small vacuum cleaner to suck up the dust.

Big dog in house. Kells at Los Alamos. Going on a boat with . . .
     Two travelers in the High Caribbean. A small gray book with soft cover. Extensively annotated in my handwriting.

Night. A bathtub in a public square.

A theater production with straight-backed chairs. Thirty people crowd in and take all the chairs. The presentation is a thriller murder story. Someone has killed his mother-in-law. I am talking to some Irish youths in a corner of the room.

Ray Masterson in Chicago. Shift to south of Spain. A blue tie with a red stain. A cat in my hotel room. Strange city squares and partitions in gold and red. Where is the beach? Someone tells me it is a taxi ride.

Hong Kong. Waiting for a boat. A huge fish in the harbor, about twenty-five feet long.

Picture in dream shows firefighters. And a lead: "Before the Big Fire of 1900." The fire went unreported in the press, but is more far-reaching than headlines of alleged events. Dream picture is similar to a folder picture.

I am trying to get back to New York. A cab would cost much more money than I have. There is a train to a place called Bush Beach.

Cat jumped off a curved cloud. Safe landing.

I attend a party and dinner at Columbia. Allen Ginsberg is there and rich. Has founded some sort of church.

Walking in strange city. Strong winds make walking difficult. I wonder how I can plan my route to get the wind behind me.

Drafted into the Army. One hundred Secret Service men there.

Nightmare. In a dark room dressed in black. My face, however, is clearly visible in white but no features can be made out. I think, Well, I am safe. Then the mirror image, a full-length mirror, reaches out black arms to me and I wake up groaning.

I am on a platform. There are three small dogs there like long-haired Pekingese. I have a small white dog or cat.

A truck rumbles by, shaking the platform. I see my little white creature lying on the platform and another dog over him. I see that he has been hit by the truck. Bend down to pick him up. Wake up sobbing.

Made it with Ian. He belongs to some esoteric group or cult. Devil worship and all.

A shoot-out. I am loading revolver and the quarry is getting farther and farther away.

Ian says: "I've been kept going by Jane Bowles and La Bronk?" (Members of the group.)

I offer to give him $30 or $35. He accepts.

Aayob is treating Mort for junk sickness.

A CIA type, a bit on the gay side. We make a long trip and he is showing me some of my own writing and some of my Egyptian glyphs. He explains that this is relative to the methadone program. In the old Empress Hotel, I meet Alan Watson. We talk and I am telling him about the CIA man and what he has said.

A tunnel which leads into a large round room with a domed top like a truncated sphere. This is the womb, and as I approach the far corner I feel a strong magnetic pull, another few steps and I will not be able to pull myself loose. I wrench free and move back

to the tunnel entrance. Here I meet Allen Ginsberg, who has a
nosebleed. Now a cry goes up: "THE DOGS THE DOGS!!"

And I realize that dogs have been released in the tunnel to force
us back into the womb. I look about for a means of escape. There
is some sort of scaffolding at the entrance to the tunnel. Could I
hold myself off the ground? No, the dogs would get up and bite my
fingers.

I see a technician . . . a dental technician. Dr. . . . . forgot his
name . . . but I recognize Charlie Kincaid. He will help me. We
are waiting on the Masks of Poseidon. These will protect us from
the dogs so we can walk back through the tunnel.

On a boat anchored on a river. I am sitting at a long table with an
old Mafia don. He is thin and elegantly dressed in a light gray suit
and striped tie. He has a pencil-line beard down the chin cleft,
which lends him a Mephistophelian air. A waiter has been sent on
some errand. The don directs him to the exit, and he falls through
a hole into the water.

I am looking at my face in the mirror. It is smooth although I
have a small pox. Some new treatment. Smallpox nights of the last
century. Stuck in the nineteenth century. Brion talking about the
office of God. Imagine thousands of years of heartbreak, seeing your
creations die.

What is the other episode that eludes me? A gunboat on the
Putumayo. The burden of dreams. Herzog. Mick Jagger. Michael V.
Cooper.

Very vivid dreams, could not believe I was not still in a dream
when I awoke, not sure where I was.

I was on a sea voyage. The passengers were all asked to take some oath to change boats and continue their journey. I and a few others refused. We were then herded aside. I was put into a small room with three bunks in it, a washstand and a toilet, bare white wall, with brutal guards, and we were supposed to stay there at least six months and would get the treatment. In charge of all this was Mary Cooke, but a younger, slimmer version, like Ted Sturgeon's wife.

At one point I was given an automatic weapon to act as guard for some natives who seemed harmless to me. An ally brought me a .32 in a holster. Next thing we are escaping in a truck through a hospital. Running into chemical apparatus and beakers and containers and out the other side. So far no hue and cry. It looks like we will make it. I remember now. No one can leave the hospital without the other half. This would seem to be what the issue was . . . only one other passenger refused, a vague middle-aged man. I never saw his face clearly, but he was in one of the bunks. The .32 was my old .32 Smith & Wesson. An Arab boy brought it to me at some point.

Three short men in front of the house. I go out and challenge them. One turns into a cat, and my hands are running with blood from his scratches.

A hotel room in the Land of the Dead, with a hamper for a window. The hamper displaces a small painting of a bilious yellow color. I put the painting back in place. Looking through the hamper, I see that there is a washbasin opposite, but the toilet and shower are at the bottom of a shaft about ten feet down. So how can I use the basin without falling to the bottom of the shaft?

Looking for a place to eat breakfast. I am sitting with Brion in hotel lobby. For some reason the atmosphere is horrible and depressing. Nobody comes to offer service, and I sit at a counter. . . . A girl comes to take my order of eggs, bacon, toast, and coffee. She doesn't seem to understand what I am saying. A man then puts a plate of soup in front of me. There are two thick stalks of asparagus in the soup, which has a faint sweet taste and is quite uneatable. The restaurant is on a platform.

I am looking for Dr. Eissler. Across from the restaurant is a row of apartment buildings and he is supposed to live there. I see a sign. I go up stairs into a very large waiting room. Am I in the right place? I should consult the directory downstairs. As I walk out, a number of elderly well-dressed Jews are coming in.

Inexplicable dream a few nights ago: Budapest . . . someone wants me to do a film script. There is a tray of candies and caramels, among others, provided by Lord Goodman. I ask about the script: "What is the Weenie?"

He shows me a sort of medallion, consisting of two pieces of metal connected by a short chain. The metal pieces were small and thin, like dog tags, and there was writing on one tag in a script unknown to me.

Gave a reading in Wichita. Five days of strenuous selection, editing, and rehearsals. Timed rehearsals paid off in an excellent reading. David Ohle said it was the best he ever heard me give. James said he was proud of me. Very good all around. Driving back in Wayne's huge van with a fridge, shower, toilet, bunks. Desolate country, burnt grass to the sky for miles. Not a house. A few straggly trees, mulberry no doubt.

I am reading *The Nigger of the "Narcissus."* Rereading or simply *reading* for the first time. Conrad establishes a meaningful relation between man and the surrounding elements—cities, jungles, rivers, and people—that science categorically denies. However, this relation is tenuous and must constantly be re-created. What he brings to the page is creative observation. I am reading the storm section in *The Nigger of the "Narcissus":*

". . . Waiting wearily for a violent death, not a voice was heard; they were mute, and in somber thoughtfulness listened to the horrible imprecations of the gale. . . . The sky was clearing, and bright sunshine gleamed over the ship. After every burst of battering seas, vivid and fleeting rainbows arched over the drifting hull in the flick of sprays. The gale was ending in a clear blow, which gleamed and cut like a knife. . . ."

At this point I stopped reading and looked out at the dreary landscape, without a touch of grandeur or spirit. Now I had moved the bookmark forward at random, to get it out of the way, and when I resumed reading I was reading the fire passage in *Youth,* and I had read a full paragraph before I realized that something was amiss. Looking out the window, I saw smoke and fire in the distance to my left. This was a grass fire, which I suppose has something to do with the crops.

A feeling of dread. Went into another room. His toenail came off. Little schoolkids. Met L. Ron Hubbard. In an empty room with the lathes and plaster showing, somehow evoking a derelict dance studio. He has a dead white face and a white suit of some wickerlike material.

"I have looked forward to meeting you for a long time."

Ian is there, with a girlfriend. Indifference on my part.

There is no beggar to equal the Screamer, who shrieks, moans, screams, and whimpers with chronic pain. You can hear him for twenty blocks. It is a terrible thing to be surrounded by a clutch of Screamers, all holding out twisted, mutilated hands.

Cabell, Dean Ripa, and Mort arrive in a car at the station. Cabell is wearing a gray suit. Mort and Dean in short sleeves. I ask Mort who is at the wheel.

"Where is the old man?"

He points across the station. I can see Dad there in a light-brown suit, standing under the clock. I walk towards him. We embrace.

James and others sitting in a circle. I am furious at being ignored. Where on earth could that have come from? So far from anything I remotely feel, it must obviously be a displacement from some other time/place context.

A pool. Two boys test the water with their feet.

"Is it cold?" I ask.

"Very cold."

I am standing on a ledge, about fifteen feet above a deep pool.

A large building, like a warehouse, reminiscent of the Raffinerie in Brussels. Fletch is there and very affectionate. A woman is carrying him as we go down a long wooden ladder, six feet to the ground.

Shift to a buffet table. There is some sort of fruit and sorbet in bowls, and I am eating from one. Seems I am supposed to give a reading, but I have no notes with me. Can I improvise? Then I notice there is no audience, except one technician fiddling with the sound system. So it seems the reading is not immediate. However, as I am handed the plate of food, I learn that the fee is $3,200.

I am split into three people. One in a gray suit that I am occupying. There is another, in a gray suit with wide shoulders, much younger . . . and a third, very young, in a sweater. I embrace him and ask if he is all right. He says in a very weak voice: "Yes, I am all right."

Now his clothes are removed from the waist down. He has undergone some sort of operation. There is what looks like a skinned penis. Also another set of genitals. I am shocked and saddened and begin to sob . . . tears dripping down onto his mutilated body.

It seems that we—James, Michael, Bill Rich, George—a few of us have indeed taken over the planet by default, occupying an empty space that no one else was able or willing to occupy. I am lying on a cot in a room with one wall missing. I say: "I will be the Sheriff."

Same dream continued another day. Like I say, we are in control, but I point out that this is precisely the most dangerous moment, since we can expect massive counterattacks from many quarters . . . CIA, KGB, Mafia, Vatican, Islam, Corporate Capitalism, the English, the Moral Majority. I propose myself as Director of Police and Counterintelligence, which will operate under one central command . . . no splitting into criminal, espionage, all that cross-purpose and confusion.

Hotel. Land of the Dead. Check to be sure I have key. Went out for dinner. Ten p.m. A Chinese restaurant. Antony Balch there. Looks like too late.

Now you see it, now you don't, unless you are very watchful.

I pass a Chinese restaurant, and I can see Antony Balch sitting at a table in the rear by the kitchen door. This tells me where I am, since Antony passed away some time ago. It also gives me an idea things aren't so good. I also gather we don't have much choice here, since Antony hates Chinese food. Any case, it is ten o'clock and the kitchen seems to be closing fast, and a menacing phalanx of waiters stands between me and the door. Everything is turned around here, you see, but they will let me through into the street again. Where is Antony? People appear and disappear here. Better get back to the hotel while it's still there. I glance at my key. There are some keys that can crumble into a gob of cold solder. And the hotel is a hole in the ground.

Woke up junk-sick with nightmare fear of a ghost. Richard Elovich goes to buy "Pinkies." It is Sunday in France. He may have to look around. I say that the only thing I have ever feared is the ghost. Whose ghost is that?

A very pale, hairless, blue-eyed cat in bed with me. It is a strange flesh-colored pinkish white. Ian and I talking to Old Man Getty. He is very friendly, talking mostly to Ian, who is better suited to understand the mysteries of shares, futures, and insider trading.

I am in a hotel. Will they send up coffee? A big studio. In the bathroom I find a cat somehow attached to the wall. I lift it down. Is it alive? There is a large montage with photographs and postcards. I am not sure whether I have done this or not. Old Man Getty disappears through a door in a scrubbed whitewashed brick wall.

Jacques Stern went out to score in Germany. Have taken a shot. Need another. A cloudlike curtain. What is it? I am going to Hong Kong to meet my family. A discreet civil servant says the temperature is 70 degrees. I am going to fly to NYC in an improvised plane. The gray curtain across the sky, and you couldn't see the mountains. This gray curtain. Alien invasion. An old Jewish woman talking to me on a portico says she likes Hong Kong better than any city except Miami. "You just know *everybody*. It's so cozy." I point out that places like that change. Tangier used to be just like that, back in the old Parade Bar days.

I have a room with a glass front on the street. I have taken a walk in a blizzard and can't find my key. A hotel in Panama with Mother and Dad. They are in room 216. I am not sure of my room number when I go down to eat breakfast. Room 218? Right.

Rambling house on the outskirts of Panama City. Crumbling walls and billboards on the housefronts. A vague area, an empty restaurant on various levels, like Le Drugstore in St.-Germain des Prés. Mother is standing below me some distance away. I am on a landing up a flight of steps. She tells me that Dr. Bradley (my veterinarian) does not advise the operation. She waves some papers and says: "The Board is confused by your rent receipts."

There are many dogs outside.

When the doorbell rang, the professor had just finished a joint in his bedroom. He had also lighted some sandalwood incense . . . a ridiculous precaution, he felt. He closed the door, and noticed that he could not see his visitor in the glass panes that occupied the upper panels of his front door. So the visitor must be small. Probably the newsboy come to collect, as he did every two weeks. The professor didn't keep track. He paid by check and was rewarded with a little tab of yellow paper.

He opened the door and there stood a small boy, dressed in strangely outmoded clothes, as if he had emerged from a Russian village.

"Hello, I'm your new newsboy." He wrinkled his nose and smiled. "And don't I smell something I shouldn't?"

The professor looked at him coldly, but he knew it was a dismal failure.

"Don't mind if I step in, do you, while you fetch the check? You see, it is *hot* outside."

The professor sat down at his all-purpose table—eating, working, receiving visitors—and wrote the check for $7.35 and handed it to the boy.

"Oh dear, I seem to have forgotten the little yellow tabs. Now isn't that careless of me? But people do get careless at times, you know. The absentminded professor? Didn't remember that he had molested a child, did he now?"

Summoning courage from some abysmal depths of the abject funk he was in, the professor grated:

"You're not me, kid."

"Well no. I find that rather hard to believe . . . and so would a lot of other people with rather rigid legalistic minds. Exactly what is *aggravated* sodomy? Now who went and aggravated that dirty old beast?"

The boy spat the words out, his face contorted with hatred. And then to the utter horror of the professor, who was at this point close to collapse, the boy unbuttoned his fly and hauled out an erection.

"You like beeg one?"

"What do you want?" the professor squeaked, like a terrorized mouse.

"What does everyone want in a capitalistic society?"

"I have no money."

"Yes you do. You got some money. And you are powerfully motivated to get more money. Child molesters don't last long in State, you know. Lying there in the exercise yard with a file up your ass. So happens I can put you in the way to make the money you're going to need."

The professor was rapidly regaining his composure. A situation clarified loses much of its terror and dread.

"I am a professor of literature. I have no access to classified materials."

"I know that, of course."

The boy gnashed his teeth in a hideously meaningful manner. Knash knash . . . he is ours. ("Knash" is the KGB code for "convert.")

Oct. 23: Date on which Dutch Schultz was shot. Dream of diving into some rather dirty water in a basement. A lake with large fish. I rocketing up into the sky. John de C. there. Talking to Bernon Woodle, who had been in Vietnam. Bitten by a dog.

Woke up in a strange room. It was very clear and vivid. Dad was there with a psychologist. I can see . . .

"Well, let me tell you, she isn't worth it."

Oh, you think, he had been actively concerned with the origin of language.

I gave an extemporaneous performance. Antony there. He says: "I would have used more nuances." Arrive at Antoine's in New Orleans.

In a South American city with James and David de C. They were going on to another city called Chillanos. I decide to stay on where I am, if the room is still vacant. The address is 77 something and I have room number 12.

Woke up hearing a little cry like a gasp of fright. (Michael reports nightmares from Halloween night. He found that his house had been burglarized . . . then the slow dread feeling that the intruder was still there in the house. His cat, Thing, sat in front of him and her eyes peeled back yellow and she started to talk. He woke up with a gasp of fear.) Sitting up in bed, I could feel the chill up the back of my neck.

I was in a hotel in the Land of the Dead. On a balcony I saw beautiful landscapes in lighter and darker shades of green. There was a valley and a hillside in front of me, with light green palm trees. A green area to the left, marshy ground with pools of water here and there, and further away to the left, a lagoon. This is Port Churchill.

A bellman tells me that Alex Trocchi wants to see me in room 24. I go to room 24 and Ian is there on a bed. Alex is sitting on a chair, I can't see his face clearly and he says nothing. Some necking with Ian that quickly turns wrong. I go away and see Ian again. Where exactly is Port Churchill?

I am walking down a street in Lawrence. I know that one man controls Lawrence, and I am contacting him. Come to a dead end, where there are bookstalls running down into basements on several levels. No one seems to be in front of the stalls, which are covered by canvas drapes and people sleeping behind. I can see way down, fifty feet, in the crevices.

I am in a boat off the pier at Harbor Beach. There are other people in the boat ahead of me. I see a small whirlpool, about two feet in diameter. Turning back, I see that whirlpools of color, red white and blue, are surrounding the boat. Why they are dangerous I don't know, but they are, and I steer back through deep black water and evade the whirlpools of color.

Bill Rich and your reporter are going shooting. We stop to pick up "Puffy" at his house, a strange, futuristic structure. On the second floor is a wide window, six feet across. I can see him up there in bed, but he does not acknowledge our call to arms. We enter a large room, open on one side, and Puffy comes down a spiral staircase, carrying a large container with a tube attached, through which he is inhaling some kind of vapor for his "Asiatic flu."

Just beyond the open side and a two-foot wall is a large lake, fifty feet deep and fifty feet wide, by three hundred feet long. The water so clear I do not at first realize it is water. Clearly, Puffy is in no condition to shoot. There is a woman there, under a plastic cover, open at both ends.

In St. Louis, in a plane flying due south towards the Jefferson Memorial on Lindell Boulevard, where the Lindbergh trophies are, I presume, still on display. I once thought of stealing them, but fortunately didn't get beyond thinking.

In the sky over the Memorial, I see an object like one of those badges carried by fake cops in Mexico: oblong, about three inches long by two inches wide, one badge piled up on another slightly smaller, so the whole device is at least an inch thick. Only this badge in the sky was about three feet long and two feet across, the colors being blue and gold. I point this out to Maurice Girodias, who is deceased, but he makes light of it.

The plane now turns west and the sky badge has shifted west and north, so it is now to the right of the plane. Looking down, I see the city is in flames, like after a bombing attack, and there is a sudden jolt and I think: Oh shit, this is it.

It is completely real, and I am trying to control my fear. I seem to be sitting in a little cubicle with a brass catch at the bottom and I think, My God if this cubicle spills open . . .

Next, with some other people I am in front of a hotel or department store. Go inside and sit down with other people in a room about the size of my front room here, like twenty by twenty . . . a number of tables and people sitting around, and I say: "How about some service?"

And people at the other table take the cue: "Yes, how about that?"

I am sitting with James and Michael and beginning to think something is not quite right. I can't remember landing at the airport, or coming here in a bus or taxi. Neither can they. And some of the guests seem to be freaking out. We obtain some guns that are obviously not in working order.

There was another "air crash" dream recently, very real, and I think, This is really it. But then land on a street.

And a number of dreams in a car or train, going very fast and expecting to crash at any moment. I experience the same real fear as I would feel in a waking situation. On the other hand, I do not hesitate to jump off high buildings or cliffs, the higher the better, knowing that I will float down. The most persistent recurring dream, almost nightly, is the unsuccessful attempt to obtain breakfast or any other kind of food for that matter, except very occasionally some utterly unpalatable dish. Usually service is rudely refused.

I am standing on a landing of an outside stairway . . . second floor. Looking through a window into a room with a slanting roof, I can see Fletch. (He is on the back porch now and I can see him through the kitchen door.) In the room are several large cats, twenty-five to thirty pounds, of a strange coloration . . . large blotches of red-purple color and black-purple. They don't seem to be bothering Fletch. On the landing is a flattened, desiccated, dusty corpse of a small gray cat, so mashed into the landing, which is gray wood, that I can barely trace the fossil outlines.

Sex scene with Mike Chase. He is kneeling naked in front of me, but on raised platform so that my face is level with his crotch. He had a semierection and everything seemed all right someway. What way? Remember a dream about Mike Chase, in a room with yellow wallpaper in an old western hotel, and I say: "Stuck in a nineteenth-century . . ."

This dream was actually Sunday, December 22. So today is Christmas Eve. And last night I was leafing through the *Audubon Book of Animals;* so many beautiful creatures . . . the Flying Fox, exactly like Fletch, and the Black Lemur. Realize how I love animals . . . mammals, that is . . . weasels and skunks and wolverines and seals and bush babies. I am turning into a latter-day Saint Francis. This morning, rescued a rat from Ginger. It is still in the house somewhere.

Obviously, the strangely colored cats I dreamed about on Saturday night were precognitions of the animals I saw last night in the book.

At a turnstile, Ian gave me some sixpence for the slot, going through himself first. I am wondering, Shall I go back and get my hat? Decide against this, for fear of missing Ian. So I click through, but Ian is nowhere to be seen, which seems odd. I proceed into a room with a round table like a library, where Mother is seated. We will take a trip . . . Mother and Ian and I, but where is Ian?

I meet Howard Brookner in the hall outside the library. We are looking down into a courtyard. What is there? I can't remember. Looking through cat pictures for a picture of Wimpy. There is not one absolutely sure, and most of the pictures are blurred or out of focus. Reading about a gang of juveniles, prowled around killing cats. What a horrible loutish planet this is. The dominant species consists of sadistic morons, faces bearing the hideous lineaments of spiritual famine swollen with stupid hate. Hopeless rubbish.

Somewhere in southern France. I have forgotten the name of the hotel at the end of the line. Find my way back and two little dogs, one gray and one black, are in the corridor and follow me into my room. These must be the Door Dogs referred to in the Tartar-dress dream. In *The Unbearable Bassington:* Comus Bassington, the image of a flawed, unbearable boyishness, at a farewell dinner. He is leaving for Africa the next day. A little black dog follows him into the dining room. Yes, it followed his father just before he was killed, thrown from a horse. Clear death omen.

The name of the hotel is Farmacía. It is way back and two little dogs also looking for a place are in the corridor. A recurrent theme. These must be the Door Dogs. Can't find suitable Comus. The image of a flawed end in a farewell dinner. He is way off base here. The next day. Streets but I can't locate France. End of the line. Subway. Christ sakes. Christ in concrete. Twenty-one little door dogs just before death definitely Comus . . . *ave atque vale.* With my black dog remember Friday. Today leading up Snap my Irish Terrier. Bowles is there. I say: "We have studied her planet of horrid black curs." Check color on the original childbirth her pathetical bones locked in the filing cabinet to the Tartar dream not sure of the door for she brings forth little me again the same misspelling follows me into my room walking word that dates back to Roman times revolution again friend about nations . . .

"What about the snails?"
  Cold feeling—nightmare fear.
  The Colonel, Civil War.
  North Dakota. He is fed up.

Orchestrate the singing.
  Make a symphony of overlapping slow-down, speed-up singing.
Run singing backward.

In the hotel, the big hotel in the Land of the Dead. Escalators,
stairways on many levels, escalators, stairways, restaurants. I
glimpse Ian several times on an escalator or passing in the corridors and waiting rooms. There is a long line of people at the
desk waiting to get rooms. I have a reservation for 317 but can't
be sure of it, with all these souls pouring in. Many of them look
American, some undoubtedly servicemen, with crew cuts and
rucksacks.
  I find Ian on a mezzanine in front of a boutique. The area is a
vast airport: train stations, docks, hotels, restaurants, film shops. He
excuses himself and goes inside. I follow after a moment and ask
a girl for Ian Sommerville. "Oh yes," she says. He comes out. A
few desultory sentences. "Is Brion here?" "No, he's not coming." I
wonder if my room is still reserved. Last night I slept on a couch
in a room with four or five other people. Booths. Several black girls.
Ian is talking shop with them, but what shop it is, I don't exactly
know.
  Wrong turnings. Track lost. Brings us to this boutique on an
alien planet. I cannot conceive of where he is at . . . home and I
am not . . . and nothing now can ever bridge the gap. He has

business of which I can have no conception. I will return to America.

Under a blue blanket I find arrowhead fragments, a yellow cat, an old motorcycle. My knees and teeth need filling. Government off to collaborate on the book with Tim Leary. Playing dice for morphine tablets.

I am on the train. Can see the Hudson. The island. Get out of a boat. Ruins of a red brick house . . . rubble and bricks and timbers . . . a bathtub. Who lived here? The Visitors will meet me here. Walking around the island. Brush . . . trees . . . rocks . . . not much. About an acre, maybe less . . . switch to Lone Star Lake. Hiatus of calm. Snow everywhere. In front of the fireplace . . . now in the room dissolving in long gray empty roads and ditches . . . moving very fast now.

Brion Gysin's birthday. Tangier has shifted to the approximate location of Halifax. It seems that cities are being moved from one place to another. Some basic planetary upheaval has taken place. I arrive in Tangier and meet Conrad Rooks. I tell him, "I have walked across Siberia. It took two months. I had to kill five people . . . New York City is gone."

I have, it seems, walked westward from the Bering Strait across Siberia and northern Europe. Got across the Atlantic and here I am.

"Who is around Tangier?" I am going westward from Tangier into empty unknown areas.

Hotel airport in London. I meet Bernon Woodle in the airport. He is going to Paris.

I have very little money, only two ten-shilling pieces and some small change. Mother is coming with money. My hotel room is in a terrible mess. Finally Allerton arrives in a very smart English topcoat, light tan with epaulets, belt, the lot. He will settle with the hotel. It seems that he is my mother.

I am in South America, trying to find a special encampment. Others will join me there. Directions are very confused. I start out and the street is fairly crowded, vaguely Latin. I look across a narrow inlet of water. I can see that the time is 12:15. (The clock looks like the moon.) The other people are supposed to join me at 1:40. I hope they know more clearly than I do exactly where. I have left my scout knife in the hotel. I decide there is time to go back for it. Pass a shop with some knives, but decide not to buy one.

Meet Jerry Evans. We sort of make it . . . at least he flashes a hard-on. Then he is driving at reckless speed down a one-way street going the wrong way. We narrowly miss a truck. Usually in dreams of fast driving, my father is at the wheel. Is Jerry my father? Hmmmmmm. The danger seems very real. No feeling that this is just a dream.

Woke from a nightmare, coughing vomit from my hiatal hernia. Back from a packing dream. Everyone *else* has luggage all packed and ready to go. Expensive cases, all leather straps and green canvas. Can't find my wallet. Look through suits hanging from pegs on the wall. Someone else helps me look and I finally find wallet in the dirty-clothes hamper. The usual commotion . . . communal dirty apartment.

Ian very friendly. I will attempt to obtain breakfast. Hope springs eternal, fella say. Ian says that my hands look like a Jew's. Most flatly insane comment I can remember. I agree. Who could deny such an allegation?

Went out to the Stone House to shoot. I lived there for almost a year when I first came to Lawrence. Now Bill Lyon, an anthropologist, lives there. He is trying to fix me up with a shaman. I want to evict the Ugly Spirit. He says Lame Deer will be here in ten days. Sure he can do more than any psychoanalyst.

There is someone there who is a former student of Bill's. I manage to coax a reasonable group of shots out of him. Back to the house for a drink, and he turns out to be a topper: everything I say, he has to top it. Invites us for a gourmet meal in Kansas City. I hem and haw about consulting my schedule. This brings up subject of food. I say, "Making curry, you season the curry a shade too hot, then smooth it out with fresh peaches or plums or honey."

"Oh yes," he says, "that's Sri Lanka curry."

Coming back in Bill Rich's freshly bought Datsun, Bill says it would be a nightmare to be trapped in that man's house. I heartily concur. An evening on his home turf might well unseat my reason, and I would be tempted to reply in kind. But it always makes me uneasy even to exaggerate any exploit, let alone falsify. I hate to lie, and I hate liars. And I know right away when someone is lying.

Remember when Gregory years ago in Paris dredged up some alleged Amazon explorer. Liars are a liability and a bore that I do not propose to bear. This explorer is full of all the Green Hell shit.

Boa constrictors swing down from trees, tarantulas big as plates, kill in seconds. "Oh yes," I tell him, "the South American tarantulas are more toxic than the American variety, but pose no danger to a healthy adult."

He huffs, "Well, you'd better go down and tell them about it, because they don't know that."

"Yeah," I say, "and the piranha fish will leap out of the water and bite a finger off, and don't even piss in them rivers, or you will be holding a bloody stump spewing piss and blood."

I figure he would look good with his head shrunked down.

Later Gregory tells me the explorer took an intense dislike to me. Wouldn't you, if you were a faker like that? . . . never saw the Amazon?

I am sitting up in bed, in white duck pants instead of pajama pants, and there are fleas on my pants, so I figure to get the Campho-Phenique and deal with this flea circus. But when I go to get the substance, I find this is not like my house in Lawrence, although the kitchen, bathroom, and door down to the basement remain intact, and part of the front room . . . but now there is a large empty room. No furniture in the front room, more like a courtyard, littered and dirty. Moreover, a gaggle of strangers is in the house now, mostly in the kitchen and what is left of the dining/living area. I tell them: "What is this? You walk in here? Ask for permission to be here, or you get out. *Now say it!*"

Some of them mutter something sullen, and seven of them walk across the front room and out the door, where they must have come in. Where am I? In Italy somewhere, I know somehow. These intruders are without distinction—not young, not old, not handsome, not ugly. One of them has a cape of some sort wrapped around him. He is one of the "walk-outs," leaving about four hard-core literary types. One of them sitting by the basement door is reading from Eugene O'Neill. I walk over to the front door and open it.

Outside is a canal with some very dilapidated wooden boats, all warped and leaky-looking, with big motors. I turn to somebody and say: "Must use up a lot of gasoline, to keep those crates floating." I am very glib and confident, and he agrees with me.

Down in the basement I find a beautiful boy. Now this boy is more than human, mutated in some way, and there is a name for such a boy, if I could bring it up to mind: an Itzigani or something . . . any case, special, same genre as the boy with the salt on his puss, but I am getting ahead of myself. This basement is something else. Bigger than the house above it. All white oak floors, white walls spreading out to the sides, with partitions and doorways. You could put five apartments down there, but it's empty now: no furniture, no doors, just white walls and floors, a shining clean white. (I glimpse the calico cat.) No dirt anywhere, and it's all mine. The boy is gone now. The basement is like an art gallery or a museum without any exhibits.

Another boy in more or less the same locale, with a canal outside. I have a rowboat and we are trying to rig a motor for it. The boy has salt crusted around his mouth, like margarita salt, and he smells of the sea and salt marshes. The rowboat was small and narrow. Never did get a motor in or launch it in the dirty, gray canal with rubbish floating by. The intruders were Italian, no doubt about that—a species of Italian clown might render the "Ha! Ha! Ha!" song, with any inducement. I didn't want to induce it. Let them take death in Venice someplace else. Got enough death right here in the Heart Land.

The Land of the Dead turned inside out.

A pension with cardboard walls and doors of paper screens. Tangier is outside . . . a few darkening streets as the lights wink out in an old film set. Can I find coffee and a roll in one of the dime cafes? This is a recurring question in the Land of the Dead. The answer is, almost certainly not. However, I find the proprietor and his wife and a few other guests grouped around a fridge in the kitchen, which is the largest room. Ian is there, looking relaxed and helpful, and brings me a slice of some bread or cake with a cinnamon flavor and color. This is remarkable. But coffee or tea seems to be much more complicated. I follow the proprietor's wife down a cardboard corridor. Folding screen leads onto the street and I make a startling discovery: Tangier is not outside.

"That isn't Tangier out there!" I exclaim.

Instead, a view across a valley and distant mountains. I enter a hall lined with cabinets of white, red, and pink ceramic patterns and arabesques of polished wood. An old woman passes an intersecting corridor in front of me, and I say "Hi" and she answers "Hi." Follow her into a room where there is food, the same cinnamon cake, and several people who seem to be quite friendly and helpful.

After breakfast in Nichols Diner (the usual, two fried eggs straight up with bacon, hash browns, toast, and coffee . . .) went over to look at Michael's apartment. Old building built to last in 1912, with a big balcony, two pull-out double beds, walk-in closets, kitchen, bath with a tub, and brick walls in the kitchen. There was a cute little gray kitten walking on the ledge of the balcony, forty feet above the street. It always makes me nervous to see a cat on a ledge like that. Suppose a bird flew by?

I break the shock of getting up and putting on cold clothes before medication. Call from Dr. Bradley, the vet, about Ruski. Seems he has some variety of feline AIDS and in any case he needs some biopsies done. I told him whatever the expense I will take care of it. He is holding Ruski overnight and I want to go visit him. I really love that cat.

Last night some species of cop is hassling me about my gun. I am carrying the .45 Ruger APC and Long Colt cylinders. I finally get a close look at him. He is wearing some sort of black velvet, tight-fitting shirt with a yellow emblem, which I presume to be his logo of authority. He has a pale thin face, and close up I can see through the lips. The teeth and gums and pale gray eyes, at once crazed and absent. It is a horrible face and I would know him again anywhere. So far as my memory serves . . . never saw him before.

Then a packing dream. I have a big suitcase and, it seems, ten minutes. I start throwing in clothes and my Kiyoga, the Steel Cobra, a spring blackjack. I hope I don't have trouble at Customs. Ten minutes. Come to think, the apartment is vaguely like Michael's apartment, with a balcony.

— ⌣ —

Met some aliens in the street and one of them gave me a pair of glasses. I am now in what looks like an optometrist's store, with mirrors and glass shelves, and find I can see everything quite clearly. The aliens form a group in Paris, and I am eating with them in a restaurant. They are not obvious aliens at first glance, but all rather outlandishly dressed in some sort of costumes, and one of them has a huge face, a foot across, on a normal-sized body. They seem to be well disposed. There are both men and women in the group. Now the bill comes, and I put in an amount that seems fair to me in some currency unknown to me. Large gray notes on parchment paper.

Mark Ewert left yesterday after a three-day visit. I feel now very much merged together. His face emerged quite clearly in a painting I did the last day he was here. He is an extraordinarily sweet and beneficent presence.

In the house at Price Road. I look down the hall and see a figure in a black monk's caul, standing at the end of the hall by the back stairs that leads down to the kitchen and the basement. Very frightened, I walk towards the figure and finally grasp it by the wrist. But it fades and slips down the back stairs, and I am trying to call to Mother in the front room: "Mother! Mother!"

But I can't get the words out. Back to my room I see a light on in the bathroom, and call out to Mother again.

The Herr Professor: "It is coming up from the basement of the mind. Up from the Id . . . the Unconscious."

I am reminded of Judge Learned Hand, who said to a lawyer

who was repeating an obvious point: "There are certain things that the Court may safely be presumed to know."

This is a figure that has appeared before in dreams, and always I am paralyzed with fear so that I cannot even cry out.

Yesterday I painted a picture called "Le Revenant," with just such a figure, in a robe that covered the head and only a black outline where the face would be.

Later, Huncke and Garver in the house. There are suitcases scattered about in the master bedroom where Mother and Dad slept. The suitcases are bound in gold, locks and hasps and straps of gold chain.

I give Huncke ten dollars in some sort of dubious currency.

Walking along a narrow street in Marrakech with Brion Gysin. The street is covered overhead, as many streets in Morocco are. There is snow in the street, about a foot deep, but it doesn't seem cold. I don't have my Gap jacket, in which I habitually carry a knife and tear gas. Don't even have my cane. However, I don't feel in danger of attack.

We are going to a meeting of some sort. Ahead of me I can see white latticework. To the right, a house back from the street. Come to a room on the right. It is a small room, about twenty by twenty, and looks like a photographic studio. The walls are paneled in some gray metal. There is a booth about six feet high, covered by a yellow cloth. A young Arab is trying to peek under the cloth. There are, I think, four people in the room when we arrive. Our meeting is in a room that opens from this room, about the same size. As I am about to go into the adjoining room, I catch the eye of a tall muscular

Arab, dressed in a light gray suit. He returns my gaze steadily and without any hostility, perhaps even a glint of understanding.

Later I find my cane.

I have an hour to pack. Can't find my all-purpose trunk, into which I can just dump everything any old way. Climb over a wooden balcony in search of this trunk, which is made of light wood. The apartment is dirty, and every closet I open is full of clothes. Perhaps I could have someone pack and send it on to me. It is a tempting idea.

In a filthy, messy apartment. My mouth is full of chewing gum. Cats have gotten into the room, over and above the cats that live here. I notice a garbage chute, half choked with food cartons, used tea bags, eggshells, orange peels. Obviously that is how the cats get in. Jacques Stern is there. Two gray anonymous young men who will accompany me on a trip. There is a stairway leading down from the apartments. As I start down the stairs, I turn towards Jacques, raising my arm in a Hitler salute like Doctor Strangelove, and sing: "We'll meet again, don't know where, don't know when, But I know we'll meet again some sunny day."

(Doomsday Machine in operation.)

A dream, years ago in Tangier, when I was living on the top floor of the Lottery Building on Delacroix Street. Ian says: "I am a woman who looks like a man. I am your dead self," and crawls away on all fours. So in the dream of last night I ask myself: Am I a woman or a man? What is this dead self? *Qu'est-ce que c'est que ce bête morte?*

It is certain that the split here is too profound for mending. No solution is viable. From De Quincey: "a chorus of female voices singing, 'Everlasting farewells.' "

How are shifts made in a dream? How does one get, say, from one room to another? By shifting the context, you are in. I am in a room at Price Road, looking out the east window. Now I am looking at a wall without windows. I am in a studio room. I know that this is a working room, and that I live somewhere else. I don't want to contact Ian, and when I see him out the window of my studio, walking on a levee, I get down on the floor so that he won't see me. However, when I walk out the door of my studio onto a landing with stone steps leading down to a road, I meet him on the steps. But is it he? Usually he is very young in dreams. Now he looks about as old as he would be if he had lived . . . that is, about fifty years old. (He was killed in a car accident in 1975.) Slender with sharp features, dressed in a light gray suit. I ask: "Are you Ian Sommerville?"

Shift to an apartment, long and narrow. A bed at one end. On the bed, a handsome boy is sitting. I sit beside him. He is dressed only in underwear shorts. We move now to a bed at the other end of the room, and I am about to make advances. But his lover, Renaldo, will arrive at any moment, and I don't want to be the cause of a jealous scene.

Knock at the door. I open it and there is Renaldo, with Ian. I say "How do you do?" to Renaldo, who glares at me coldly. Walk down some steps with Ian. Ian says Renaldo is one of the Benvenuto Beach crowd.

I have what I suspect to be a live cockroach stuck in my ear. I can't see it fully in the mirror. This is in the usual dirty pension, and Michael Portman refuses to look at it or attempt to dislodge it. I lose my temper and push him on a landing and he falls down.

I am involved in some fraudulent scheme in Canada to market some drug to cure alcoholism. The company chairman is reading into a telephone or microphone. "We are at war. We are under siege." Nobody about in this great empty building . . . dusty and dirty but large. I have been promised $128 to write some blurb for the company. I say: "I haven't been paid!" Then a woman comes into my room that opens off a large hall and gives me $500, she says. It looks like stage money. I can't even find any numbers on the lower-denomination, one-dollar bills. Figure I'd better ask the bank if the notes are genuine before I try to cash it.

Meanwhile the police have arrived in huge vans, high as two house stories, and everyone crowds to the window, looking down onto the street. Looks like Lower Broadway seen from a second-floor loft. Brion says: "Well, we can stay here for a hundred and five dollars per month and the directors will beat any charges, because they are Elliots."

He needs to conserve his Sek. They call it "ammo" here. The Sek has to be pure or it won't discharge. Essential to avoid the deadly distractions: sentimentality which is secondhand affect, "made in Hollywood" self-glorification. Then he starts saying: "Looka me! Looka me!" You have to look fast. He won't be there long. Like waving around a .25 in a room full of .45s. The survivor doesn't want to be looked at. Doesn't want to be seen. By the time he is close enough to be seen, there won't be anybody to see him.

I harbor deep distaste for scientists. Give me a worldly cultured priest any day, and twice on Sunday . . . and not some timorous old beastie, cowering in the eternal lavatory of a dead universe.

"Dreams mean nothing," Crick croaks, "just neural housecleaning. The quicker we forget our dreams the better." He's telling me *my* dreams, where I get my best sets and characters, are meaningless. Meaningless to whom, exactly? They can't even think straight. As if "meaning" floats about in a vacuum, with no relation to time, place, or person. Science is as riddled with underlying dogmas and outright falsifications as Catholicism. More so, in fact. The most basic dogma is that the human will cannot possibly produce any physical effects. "No death wish can ever be effective." No? Anybody who keeps his eyes open sees people wished to death all the time.

"No one seriously says that the rituals of a shaman can produce any changes in the weather." Quote is from an article in *New York Times.* Don't recall writer or subject. He has obviously swallowed the implicit dogma hook, line, and blinkers. I have seen weather magic. I have even performed weather magic.

It follows from the above-mentioned dogma that ESP *must* be invalid. One scientist said he would never believe in telepathy, no matter what evidence he was offered. John Wheeler takes up arms against ESP, complaining that he has enough trouble observing his fucking photons without ESP buzzing around his ears, and signals transmitted faster than the speed of light.

That nothing can exceed the speed of light is another scientific dogma, more hallowed and inviolate than the Immaculate Conception or the Holy Ghost. So I flick a switch and a light goes on or off, ten light-years away. "Impossible to exceed the speed of light."

Don't have to. Simple matter of synchronicity. After all, we've come a ways since the Rothschilds got dirty rich from signals reflected on mirrors across the channel to France. One is way beyond such primitive cause-and-effect modes of communication. In fact, the whole concept of communication is antiquated.

Another inviolate dogma is mortality. "The only thing that gives dignity and meaning to life is death," said an English physicist. He's shoving it down all our throats, not "from my viewpoint" or "my opinion," but THE ONLY. The Hallowed Mould, or you might call it the Immaculate Rot.

This English one I read in a book review years ago, and here is John Wheeler, only yesterday: "There is no picture without a frame. No life without death." Same song, but not so clearly stated. Perhaps Wheeler did not have the advantage of a classical education.

What have I done in my life? Scratched a few surfaces. Not ready to be framed yet.

Severe pain last night and this morning. Left side, down the left arm and up into the jaw. Classical heart attack symptoms, but a previous attack was diagnosed by Dr. Gray as emphysema . . . a bubble bursting in the lung. Painful, but not dangerous. However, Dr. Gray misdiagnosed James' classic appendicitis. Fortunately, Michael got him to the emergency room in time. So I think it is time to seek a second opinion. Will call the other doctor tomorrow.

I have been to a concert with Kerouac and others. What others? Where? I can't remember. What time is it? Six o'clock? Have I had breakfast?

A large dusty room like a loft. Sitting now at a table. Some strawberries and sugar on a plate. A shift, a bag on the table. I extract
a chocolate-covered confection shaped like a scarab, two inches
long and an inch thick. I bite into it. The inside is white, creamy,
with a taste of coconut, marzipan, opera cream, inhumanly delicious
with a tingle of glancing sweetness. I know I can eat the whole bag
and then want more more more, consumed by insatiable craving. I
can sit there and eat and eat until the toothsome tangy cream dis-
solves my teeth and bones down to a churning, slobbering maw of
ravening hunger.

A rowboat in a lake or a lagoon. The water is gray and dead calm,
slick as glass but still the boat is moving farther and farther out
until I can barely see the shore. There must be a current like a
surface river. Gray sky now, and gray water to the horizon.

Find myself in ancient Rome talking to Cicero, who complains
that the situation is unstable and dangerous. He would prefer a
little peace. He has a long nose, like a figure in a painting I did
yesterday, and I notice now that the figure, which is black on white,
has a suggestion of a toga.

There is a room where no females are allowed. This is a permanent location, you might say, no females in here ever—and when
I go in, I am leaving the whole male/female world forever. Eternal
farewells. There is a serving bar between this room and the area
where I am. Some women are sitting there, and I say: "Stand aside!"

They do, and I climb over the bar, but behind me I can hear
other female voices saying that they do not agree to my departure.
The room into which I have climbed is small like the kitchen here.
But there is a door beyond. The voices still complaining from the
outside area.

Another set dream. In a room sitting at a wood table with several other people I can't remember. At one end of the room is a pool of stagnant water. Now a basket of the deadly confection is brought from the floor and placed on the table. What looks like brown eggs with thickened shells, little tubes and curls in caramel brown and creamy white. I bite into an eggshell. The same intolerable aching sweetness . . . toothache sweetness.

Then someone comes in with a gun he is making. The barrel is not yet drilled and the side is open, spilling incomprehensible springs and screws and polished steel parts.

I think it was before Toronto, why do I keep saying Seattle? I am standing in the usual dream set of a large dirty gray loft and a messenger in a slovenly dirty blue uniform with peaked blue cap has a message for me which is diverted by someone else claiming to be me and taking the message. Then another messenger arrives . . . old, with wrinkled yellow parchment skin like a mask showing under his cap, and this time the message is a visiting card with my name on it, all smudged and dirty . . . no dodging this one. *The Postman Always Rings Twice.* Yes, it was just before leaving for Toronto and not precisely an auspicious omen.

Then a dream, first night in Toronto at the Sutton Place Hotel in my luxurious suite. I am at a station and the train comes by and stops only a few seconds, no time to get on, and they are open at the sides like cattle cars. I finally board one and it stops at ARMY POST and everyone gets off. It's the end of the line. I find a mac-adam road leading down and ask someone if this road will take me to St. Louis. He says yes. How far? "About six miles." I figure I can make it in an hour, being all downhill. Some sections of the road are like a market, with vegetables and fruits and people milling around.

Several terrific attacks during the five days I passed in Toronto. Excruciating pain, radiating down the left arm and up to the jaw. Popping nitro pills like peanuts. It comes in waves and nails you down. No way to detach yourself since there is no place to detach yourself to. Bill Rich met me in K.C. and saw me through. Back through a hailstorm (tornado warning), Tuesday late afternoon. Hail like golf balls. The insurance companies had to pay out millions for dented cars and fractured roofs.

Saw Dr. Hiebert on Thursday after Toronto and straight to the hospital. Dye X-rays showed major artery ninety-eight percent blocked. Angioplasty Monday morning. Left St. Francis Hospital in Topeka on Tuesday afternoon. A very close thing. Dr. Hiebert said he should not have allowed the Toronto trip. I had no idea just how serious the situation was. Another three or four days and . . . massive heart attack.

I think a lake in Nevada. I could see boats out a window. Last night a Visitor dream. Heard people talking in front room. Mort was there. Then I, Snubbie in hand, stepped out of bedroom and there were two men standing in the doorway to the front room. I went into the front room. Bedstead gone. A man in a red costume was lying on the floor and said something insulting. I said: "I could never shoot anyone without reason." There was a woman who was formed from white porcelain from the waist up. She is cavorting around. A man who announced himself without saying anything as a *Visitor* and leader of the group said: "You are causing trouble. You have too many irons in the fire." His face is gray and anonymous. His upper lip does not move when he talks but I can see gray teeth. Fletch, who is on my bed, says something enigmatic. There is a reference to Ted Morgan and a filter cigarette, half smoked in ashtray.

Looking for breakfast in the Land of the Dead. Before, Kells and Dick Seaver together. I am annoyed with Kells. I don't remember why . . .

Now out in front of hotel looking for breakfast. I seem to be in Italy. The whole area is like the deck of a huge ship. I am ready to settle for bread and coffee, but can't seem to get the attention of the waiter. Now the ship is moving. I don't know where we are going, and I keep asking: "Where is this ship going? Outward bound?" I finally find out we are headed for England and I am furious with James for having deceived me as to the destination. I look at him across the deck. I have only two dollars. It is four o'clock in the afternoon. I glare at James. Where is this ship *going*? For some reason I don't want to go to Italy, and I tell James, "When we get to London we go to separate hotels. Then I am going home." What can I do in London? Visit some pop stars or what? Why am I annoyed with James? What is wrong? The ship is not heading out to sea . . .

My apartment in NYC, if it can be so designated, is open on two sides, more like a corridor or a covered street. I am packing, going to St. Louis or anywhere west of New York. There is something terribly wrong here, like a plague, some imminent disaster that hangs in the air like a haze. My clothes and toilet articles are packed into a small gladstone bag. Three handguns I have put aside on a shelf behind a curtain. It will, I decide, be dangerous to travel with handguns in my luggage. In any case, I can easily buy a gun in St. Louis when I get there, if I get there. My suitcase is on a low shelf by the wardrobe. I open a drawer and find some more belongings; a pair of scissors, a handkerchief, socks . . . well, no time to bother.

My friend Ira Jaffe, now a resident doctor in a New York hospital, is there. He doesn't seem concerned. We walk down to a square surrounded by concrete walls stained with rust and graffiti. A group of men is gathered there, a disreputable-looking bunch with the look of petty criminals, loafers, ward heelers, police informers . . . but Ira greets them in a friendly and familiar manner and invites them back to our digs, where they snoop about, whispering to each other and smiling. After they leave, I turn on Ira.

"Ira, do you *know* those people?"

"Well, I know one of them . . . sort of."

"Why the hell did you invite them here? They have probably seen the guns and will go straight to some cop they know. They look like copper lovers."

"Well . . . uh . . ."

Furious, I decide to leave my suitcase and the guns and travel in the worn brown suit I have on.

We walk out together. I see a crowd of people milling around the bus station, queues winding out to the street. Ira goes in to make inquiries.

"All buses going west of New York are full for twenty-eight days. Same with boats going to Puerto Rico. All planes are grounded indefinitely."

I see now that there is a beach by the bus station, and I start looking for a train station, up steep wood stairs that end in a wooden door with a rusty iron ring. I pull the door open. It leads down into a dark warehouse.

The whole city looks unfamiliar . . . gray buildings, walls, steps going down. I come to an open-air market in a square about a hundred feet on each side . . . booths and stalls, produce. I notice strawberries, flowers, tomatoes. In a corner of the market several men are gathered. Workmen, I assume, connected to the market. I demonstrate that I can levitate, but they pay no attention. I pick one man and lift him off the pavement.

"Look down . . . see? We're floating."

I put him down and see that he is violently hostile. I try to placate him.

"Most people are bewildered and much impressed. You are a rare exception."

He smiles a ghastly, insulting grimace that goes on and on, more and more insulting, portentous, inhumanly hostile, a smile of pure inhuman hate. He is about thirty, thin, pale, dressed in a dirty-blue jacket and pants that suggest a uniform of some significance, remote and inexplicable as his snarling, implacable hate. He is standing now by a rack that contains tools . . . a hammer, chisels, an adze. There is a vise attached to a shelf and a bottle of some red-colored soft drink.

Now a man like a floorwalker approaches, big feet, black suit and shoes. A smooth waxy face and protruding round eyes. I levitate him, and he seems properly impressed. I expect at any moment the enemy one will attack me with one of the tools while my back is turned. I whirl around and do something that is, in hindsight, completely inexplicable. I see only the action itself, without any discernible affect or motivation. I pick up the bottle and break it against the vise and ram the broken, jagged glass into his face, and walk rapidly away. He is following about thirty feet behind me, holding a hand up to his bleeding face. I realize that I have done a hellish thing, and that he will follow me from here to eternity holding a bloody hand to his face.

So why did I ram the broken bottle in his face? Well, he was hostile and dangerous. Sure was, and with good reason. (Remember me? End of the line in Brooklyn? And recently, too, remember the shabby little man in some sort of vague blue uniform and peaked cap? Presented you with a summons you might say, a dirty smudged visitor card with your name on it? It was just before you went to Toronto to boost the film and came near to a massive heart attack.

So what do you suppose that meant, that card with *your name* on it? "And who do you think I am, Western Union?" And before that, remember produce along the road?)

Here we are in plague-stricken New York? Airborne AIDS, is it? And you figure to levitate your way out. Or St. Louis encephalitis by birth and nickname? And you come to this market occupies a square block, produce, *strawberries* . . . Now, the strawberry in Bosch talk means deadly fucking lust. Sort of thing could lay a man open to a world of hurt. So here you are, and here he is, and you shouldn't be here at all, which is bad enough, but to really stick it in and break it off, you have to pick him up and waltz him around in the air. And *then* you wonder why he is hostile. I never hurt the guy. We should get together and talk about our *relationship* like a couple of Vassar girls.

Here he turns up months later in a painting, one eye missing, face horribly scarred. One eye missing, face black with hate, what looks like an acorn growing out of the side of his face . . .

Last night, dream of a crowded cafeteria—not crowded really, just about twelve people, who cluster in behind me in rather an insolent and threatening manner, like twelve treacherous Disciples. We come to the food counter, hardly anything there. I point to a bun and say, "Tea and a bun?" I repeat several times: "Tea and a bun," "Tea and a bun." The girl is not behind the counter and now a male attendant closes in on me. I have done something awful, he is going to eighty-six me, and I push *back* and wake up. Repeat, here is a messenger of DEATH, considers himself very important, and you pick him up and expect him to like it? Well, he doesn't like it. Doesn't like it at all.

So you want to fix it with him. "What's your name, boy?" (I am known for my exquisite tact. Why can't folk understand that I really *mean* well?)

At this point I pick up a piece of paper, and it is the first draft of an obituary that I wrote for Arthur C. Chase who taught English at Los Alamos Ranch School, went on to teach at Berkshire School, and has recently died.

"Hmmm, well, Chase is good as any. I've been called harder names, and it won't hurt my feelings."

"Any case, I gotta keep my books straight . . . Remember when you worked in the accounting department of Inland Rubber, and balanced your books by altering the inventory? Haven't gotten their books straight to this day . . . ? So I'm short a card."

Consider now other dream encounters. The officer on the ship (again the vague uniform that designated some unknown authority). He questioned my statement that I was a writer, because I was found in dubious company . . . Remember in the end of *Naked Lunch* film, Lee proves he is a writer by making something happen, by shooting his wife? So here I am, not writing very well by myself. Should be first-class at least.

"Tea and a bun? Tea and a bun?" What kinda writing is that? Get him out of the company cafeteria. You're not allowed seconds. And to go way back to Pine Valley and the dream driver of a tractor, was it, I said something to him when he grazes me and he looks back and accelerates his vehicle in reverse and tries to run right over me. "Get in my way, will you? You were making a filthy noise."

Typewriter starts growling like a nasty spirit . . . "The room is slowly filling up with evil spirits," and the nicer I am with them the eviler they get. Like Christ say, you throw out one evil spirit and her will come back with seven more wicked than itself.

— ◡ ◡

Now for the chow dog at the end of the street.

I will simply walk up and shoot it with my .38 Snubbie as I intone:

"You have a black tongue!"

And all the neighbors will applaud my act in eliminating this vile, black-tongued abortion, this Oriental freak, this alien swine dog . . . an abomination to God and Lawrence.

So the Mayor herself will award me the Red Cross for Bravery and the keys to the city. And I will vow to prevent a second coming of Dog Quantrill.

It often happens in a dream that two or more narrative lines are happening at the same time, but one intends to impose sequential structure so that one follows the other.

I am on a train. Allerton passes me going towards the back of the car in the other direction. He looks very young and handsome dressed in a light-brown suit. I call out: "Allerton!" but he doesn't hear me because of the train noise. So I get up and start after him. Into the next car, but I don't see him, and the car ends in a seat that runs all the way across. So I turn around and start back.

I am on a train going back to St. Louis. I have been drafted into the Army as a private and I am in uniform. I feel very disgruntled. How can they draft a man of seventy-two? The doctor has made a mistake. It is ridiculous. I have a feeling of having come full circle, back to this dreaded point. The train stops and I get out, walking under an arcade. I realize now that I don't have my passport with me.

I walk out of the station. There is a square in front of me and mountains in the background. Looks like Colorado Springs. Just back from my search for Marker. There are long bunks along both sides of the car at the top. There are young boys in the bunks, all returning from school somewhere.

I walk into a large room like a gymnasium behind the train. The room is empty. I see some canes in one corner but when I go to look at them, they are gone. There is a closet or locker and a pair of high shoes.

Back on the train. There is a long ride and absolutely nothing to do. How can I endure the time? A feeling that there is nothing outside the train gives me a terrible sense of being enclosed in nothingness.

Back in the room, which opens into another room. "An overwhelming feeling of universal damage and loss." Just the shoes he used to wear. Dust and mold, and nothing outside the room.

I am groaning with grief and desolation.

"Oh my God. Nothing here. Nobody here. Just the empty shoes."

Whose empty shoes?

An apartment located on top of a truncated stone pyramid about fifty feet aboveground. I see that there is an apartment under this one and I can see down an outside stair or ramp in a blue-green light.

Now I am in the lower apartment, in a bedroom with a naked boy who says: "You and I are just old sluts."

He has a strange body, perhaps four feet tall, with white skin and slightly hairy on the stomach, with broad shoulders and thin hips. The face I cannot see clearly. There is an electric element, as if I am trying to activate some very complex device which I don't fully understand.

Someone in another bedroom. When I visit him, he stands in the doorway blocking my way, obviously because he doesn't want me to see who is in the room with him. I don't care, and I say so. He is standing directly in her path, seconds to countdown. As her bowels give way and yellow shit trickles down her legs and splatters on the floor, she emits a wail of distress like an animal's wail. (In fact she had a nervous breakdown shortly afterwards.)

Shitting woman.

Now I recollect Bill Simpson's wife had this unfortunate condition. At any moment she could start to fart and shit uncontrollably and rush from the room, and all the guests were mostly upper-class English faggots and they would all outdo each other at ignoring the incident, going right on with what they were saying, just a shade louder to drown out the farts—just the *right* shade louder, and never as much as one raised eyebrow or even dropping the ash off one cigarette.

The only reason anyone tolerated Bill Simpson was that his shitting wife was loaded with it up the ass and he had a big comfortable villa on the Riviera, all stocked with distinguished lunch and dinner guests, why even the Duke and Duchess of Windsor turned up, looking like escapees from a Swedish insane asylum, 1920. So the English Edel Fags made a stop there. They were discreetly indoctrinated: "Just pay no attention." And like I say, outvied each other in discretion.

It was after lunch, everything quiet, soon they will drift off for a siesta, when it hits. Audrey was more than up to the occasion. He produces a roll of toilet paper from a hidden pocket . . . and a great big boyish smile.

"Can I help you, lady?"

Standing right in front of her, blocking the way, so she turned loose with a stream of diarrhea down her legs, dripping onto the floor.

Then he snarls in her face like a dog: "Uncontrolled slut!" and fetches her a crack across the chops, knocked the spit out of her mouth. And no Colonel there to horsewhip the cad.

Well, to tell the truth, Mrs. Simpson was a real pain in every-body's ass, and some muttered that she did it at times that suited her bitchy purposes, for she hated all Bill's airy-fairy friends. "Oh look what just flew in . . ." she would greet them.

So they just sat there. But Bill *had* to do something, you see it was HER money, and she wasn't such a fool as to put *anything* in his name. (If there is any sorrier spectacle than a queen who has married some disgusting dog for her money . . .)

"Get out of my house, you young, young . . ."

Audrey shrugged. "Cad, bounder? Doesn't quite make it, though."

Meanwhile she has escaped, leaving a puddle of yellow shit on the floor. Audrey calls to the Arab servant: "Why don't you housebreak the old shit-bag? It's bloody disgusting. She was making a filthy noise."

Spit runs down Bill's chin. He casts an appealing glance at the butler. Audrey throws the roll of toilet paper, hitting the butler in the chest.

"Well, clean it up, you worthless old fart."

The butler is unperturbed.

"Ddddddddddddddooooooo sommmmething!" Bill stammers.

"I am giving notice, sir. I was hired as a butler, not a lavatory attendant or a bodyguard." He bows stiffly and leaves the room.

Audrey exits after him, emerging two seconds later with a col-lapsible moped: Sput sput sput.

Bill looks around at his guests, five in all: "Getttt ouuuut of myy hhhhouse!"

"Glad to, old sod."

"Confidentially, it stinks."

"And sucks."

"My best to the old shit-bag."

The fifth man is something special. He gives Bill the finger and ejects his false teeth, which bite Bill on the nose. Bill slaps at them, but they have locked. As the fifth man walks by him, he opens his mouth like a jewfish and pulls in the teeth, which tear loose and snap back into his mouth, leaving Bill alone and bleeding hysterically.

Bill falls sobbing across the sofa as the curtain falls.

Toilet is flushed offstage.

Last night in an apartment, more like a corridor, open on one side to the street. I saw a boy I knew ride by on a bicycle, and other boys across the street, and felt very lonely. I was working on a book—painting. After every sentence there was a column to the right with the word "bite." "Please," but I was sharing a room with Mother at the end of the hall, and her had to sleep, so I couldn't work on the book anymore.

Michael Portman was in a room at the end of the hall, separated by a curtain. Later I saw some boys sneaking into my room and I knew they were there to steal my .38 Snubbie.

Dream shifts are not at all like a film with fade-outs and all that jazz. More a shift of viewpoint: John Cooke's apartment, and there is Mary Cooke looking slim and stylish, except her legs are thick and gross. We make conversation. I ask if she has been to Marrakech lately. Then John is talking into a phone to Brion, arranging to go to an Armenian church to hear a Gregorian chant: "Oh, very special." And Mary Cooke is gone, and we are out on Eighth Street in NYC. John's getting into a cab, and Brion is walking away and says over his shoulder that his address is 121 or 122 York Street.

Meanwhile a drunken professor I know from someplace has approached me. Shall I have a drink with him and his girlfriend? It seems like a bad idea, fraught with disagreeable potentials.

Bitten by a monkey creature with tiny teeth.

My Press Releaser Kim Carson said: "The only goal worth striving for is immortality." And fuck the physicists who say: "There is no picture without a frame. No life without death. Why, the only thing that gives life meaning and dignity is death. Why should there be another life? Don't you get enough here?" Indeed, yes: enough bullshit.

Now there are two routes to immortality. They might be designated as: slow-down or speed-up, or straight-ahead or detour. Reference aphorisms of the Old White Hunter. In the time that you face death directly, you are immortal. That's the straight-ahead route. The slow-down detour vampire route—take a little, leave a little, sure, skim a year off a thousand citizens, they won't know the difference—but what happens when you run short of citizens, which you will sooner or later? Also, speed-up route is a kill route, whereas slow-down is a manipulate, degrade, humiliate, enslave route.

So how does one face death head-on? . . . without flinching and without posturing—which is always to be seen as a form of evasion, worse than flinching, because covert. For the man who flinches and runs away, like Lord Jim and Francis Macomber, there is hope. But not for him who sticks out his chest and wraps himself in a flag, a Gallic shrug from the French naval officer in *Lord Jim,* one of the great characters of fiction:

"Parbleu, il s'en fuye, mais il a laissé son cadavre en place . . ."
"He has run away but left his carcass behind."
"Intrigué par ce cadavre?"
"Intrigued by that corpse?"
Not really . . . a well-known and documented schism, something familiar about that figure moving farther and farther away. "Why! Himself!" Like the song say, "They don't come back, won't come back, once they're gone . . ."

Sitting on a sloping deck with two companions in traditional hippie garb of filthy jeans, long straggly hair, and knapsacks. I myself am more conservatively attired, in a suit and a tie. This is, it would seem, steerage class. Two customs officials are questioning my companions. One is typical, slightly paunchy, gold teeth, mustache. The other is obviously the educated one, in a gray suit and black tie. He has a long protruding oval face, gray skin, pale gray eyes. I tell him that I am a writer, and he *smiles,* a smile reflecting incredulity, hate, contempt: obviously, I could not be a writer in the company of "heepies."

There is something else, and now I recognize him as the guard in the Market, in the dream where I am trying to get out of plague-ridden New York City and shove a broken bottle into his face. Something else in the smile. I can't write the smile, there are no words for his smile. And now it escalates, showing more and more of what? His whole face lights up with it. I realize that he is *sick* . . . sick to death with some horrible illness. That smile is pure evil, so pure it fucking *shines.*

"Where we are is Hell, and where Hell is, there must we ever be."

So now I see the boat, which is about 150 feet long, low in the water, of a gray-green color, looking like a destroyer. I have left my luggage in the hotel and decide I will not go back. I have, in the dream of traveling in steerage, a small gladstone bag, which will establish my credentials as a writer, containing one of my books. I keep telling Smiler to send for it.

A series of my paintings is based on the mystery of the *Mary Celeste*. The brigantine *Mary Celeste* was sighted under full sail off the Azores in 1872. A boarding party found the ship deserted. (One lifeboat and the ship's compass were missing.) The cargo of alcohol was untouched. The ship left Halifax for Lisbon with a crew of thirteen. The captain's wife was on board. The *Mary Celeste* was towed to Gibraltar, where a board of inquiry was held.

A number of theories were advanced. Pirates? Then why was the cargo untouched? Alcohol, as cooking fuel or to fortify wines, is readily saleable in the area: Spain, Portugal, Morocco. Sea monsters? Ergotism? Perhaps alien abduction? After reading *Communion* and *Breakthrough* by Whitley Strieber, I became seriously interested in alien landings and abductions. I visited him and spent a weekend at his cabin. After talking with him and his secretary and reading the *Communion Newsletters,* I was convinced that the aliens, or whatever they are, are a real phenomenon. The abductions, in several accounts, involved sexual contacts. Indeed, that would seem to be their purpose.

On my way to Europe on a boat. I am in a large dormitory, a bed by the wall. A little creature attaches itself to my back. I pull it around where I can look at it. The creature is cat-sized and resembles a humanoid octopus. It has a round disk mouth, about an inch to an inch and a half across, equipped with suction pads, about one third of an inch across. It also has, I think, four tentacles, each about a foot in length. It keeps trying to reattach itself. I can see no eyes. The creature seems to be blind, and perhaps wants to use my eyes. Someone tells me that these creatures are particularly prevalent in the beds by the far walls nearest the sea. I feel no repulsion for the creature.

Then a man about forty years old, with a high forehead and a black toothbrush mustache, sits down opposite me, looks into my eyes, and says in a slimy, obscene, insinuating voice: "Celestial Babies!"

Which I interpret as a reference to the *Mary Celeste*. Inference being that the abducted crew of the *Mary Celeste* had sexual relations with the abducting aliens, and these "Celestial Babies" were the offspring.

I am going to France on a boat with David Budd. We have third-class accommodations, which is a cubicle like his sleeping place in his loft at 333 Park Avenue South. On the flimsy door, a flimsy padlock. I don't like it. I want first-class accommodations, and go to a large room where ticket assignments are consummated.

I see a long line of incredibly ugly people, a man grossly fat, a thin one with a long neck, like parodies of people in drawings by Grosz. And to the right, a desk with no line for the first class. I tell a man at the desk I want first class, and he says I will have to pay a supplement of $638. I only have about $130. So I slide away, hoping they will not ask payment at once, and perhaps I can have the money sent from home or use my checkbook.

I sit down for dinner in a seat at a counter. I am the only one there, apart from waiters who bring me an incredibly awful meal.

Starter consists of a bowl of cold water with a few shreds of wilted lettuce and pieces of cold ham and beef and veal floating in the water. I ask what is the main course and the waiter says it is "dressing." I order some red wine, with no real expectation of getting it.

Going over the boat, I come to a room with about thirty people with babies on pallets. This is strange. A large second- or third-class room has a number of people and cats, a large long-haired black cat about three feet long, another cat with a small head almost like a chicken, and a dog lying back in a baby carriage.

On a bus, but still on the boat. Two boys come in. They are very thin, in pressed gray suits and ties, with incredibly smooth, pale faces, the lips pale and smooth as if there is no blood in them. Their bodies are not more than a foot across the shoulders, and about four inches through. They say nothing, just stand there. Outside, I can see trees and hills; we are passing land.

(Tainted fish from Danger River.)

Outside, I can see a landscape. We are passing quite close, perhaps through a channel, but I can only see out the right side of the boat. The landscape is clearly the Azores. (I passed them once, going to or from Tangier.) The Azores are completely different from the usual Mediterranean landscape of olive trees, scrub, thistles, and stony beaches: a green pastoral picture of trees, meadows, cultivated fields, stone bridges, and stone houses. The green fields extend right down to the water's edge, with no beaches in sight, as if the island had been lifted from somewhere and put down there.

A Celestial Baby turns into Fletch and snuggles against my chest purring.

"Hold me! Hold me! Hold me!"

Aching sadness . . .

Suddenly Fletch jumps up. There was a sound, it seems.

I have been sitting there twenty minutes . . . hold me hold me hold me . . . and the sadness, not easy sad but wrenching, tearing sad, and devotion to his charge, devotion of the Guardian . . . the alertness, the searching probes, feeling for danger spots, splashes and blurs of old, vague, forgotten plots to put some desiccated fraudulent pretender on a dispossessed throne before Household Finance hauls it away to a warehouse full of "or else."

Celestial Babies can take any form that the Guardian can see: lemur, cat, monkey, flying fox, or any creature of dream and fantasy.

Black storm clouds cut by flashes of silver light, a green flash on the skyline. Glimpsed a sail in the distance, bright and clear for a moment, then wiped away by a veil of rain.

None of this happened, or rather it happened at the same time as the watches and meals and entries in the logbook, tomorrow and tomorrow of not seeing beyond the illusion of present time.

A painted ship, a painted ocean, a phantom crew going through the motions of watches, meals, entries, in the logbook six miles off Santa Maria, simple men, plain pleasures. There was no security in the alligators. Where are you all going? *Quo vadis?* To Gnaoua, with alcohol to fortify their wines.

The artist sees something invisible to others, and by seeing and recording it on canvas, makes it visible to others.

So the function of the painter is to observe and make visible in paint something that did not exist until he observed it.

A meaning-sensitive observer creator who observes what a manifestation *means* . . . means to whom, or what? To the observer. He may find himself beset by larval beings, desperate to be observed and to exist by being observed.

But he could see it all, the *copains*, the abusive letters and critics. He could win through to doddering fame and lily ponds with a housekeeper to keep pests away from the Master. He knows how these things are done.

Or a writer . . . his face bears scars of the early struggles, the years of neglect and scorn from the critics . . . but just hold the line and you will be the grand old man of letters, with your napkin ring in a very special discreet restaurant. Perhaps even the Academy. Why not? He knows the routes, the favors exchanged, the causes espoused, the faultless manner, the flowery inscriptions.

Or he could have dived into the underworld, sleek and swift and deadly as a barracuda. He would always know who was his enemy before the other knew it. That is the secret: always be there first.

Well, let us contact the Muse. Come in, please . . .

Egypt. What am I doing here? It's terrible. I can't stand to be living in lodging houses with hostile innkeepers. They all hate me on sight, as do all dogs. I have to get out of this nightmare. But how? We will go upriver to Memphis to find the old Gods—terrible old frauds most of them, but some did have some items of value. Here is an amulet from Bast the Cat Goddess. There is also a male cat-God amulet. All dogs hate and fear it, for it brings the ancient hate into the open. What is a master of ten enraged cats?

He had achieved a modicum of serenity in Alexandria, but the dogs made his life a hell. Then he got two bodyguards with heavy clubs, but even this was not enough and they frequently had to use their short swords. Finally he captured a wild cat. He nurtured it and it became his cat. It rubbed itself against him and jumped into his lap.

Now it is time. He releases the cat and points to the dog. The cat streaks towards the target and leaps on the dog and tears its guts out.

In a hospital with nurses. They have just brought my dinner, which consists of two large chickens covered with gravy and a slice of pie. I have eaten one whole chicken with stuffing when I decide to make a phone call. When I turn back to my bed the tray is gone. I am still hungry and furious, protesting to the nurses that I wasn't finished. What about the pie? James is there and we are both trying to talk her into bringing our food back.

I notice two strange animals like ferrets from my Half Human section in *The Place of Dead Roads*. Houses boarded up, others have an air of being semioccupied. On a porch a rusting bicycle is overgrown with morning glory vines. From one house drifts a heavy odor of flowers and the musky smell of impossible animals—long, sinuous ferretlike creatures that peer out through bushes and vines with enormous eyes.

I tell James that we are undoubtedly at a nuthouse. Just exactly to what extent we are confined is difficult to say.

Scene shifts to a school for psychic studies. I talk to a young man with a little beard who mistakes my interest for sexual attraction, and says that the way I am coming on to him raises doubts as to whether I can be entrusted with such knowledge. He has fine, straight hair, like an Indian or Japanese, and I recognize him as a certain type character who can never be convinced that one is not sexually attracted to him.

In McAllen or Pharr, Texas. Brion and David Budd there. I am watching visions on the wall. A boulder with a tree growing beside it. An encampment like Bedouins in Technicolor, purple and red and yellow light and robes.

Mother there in car.

Shift to a hotel.

"The Rothschilds are back."

Jacques down the hall with Gregory. A drink in the bar with Alan Watson. David Budd there. I say: "I'll have one more."

In a car with James on a two-way road with island in middle. James crosses the island in front of another car and puts us into a spin in front of the car, then speeds, off at terrific speed, the other car in pursuit. He outdistances the car across an area of cracked concrete where white butterflies are everywhere.

Finally we drew up in front of the house and went in, and I found a .32 revolver in a drawer. Now the two occupants of the other car came in and I covered them with the gun, and they both turned into little half-grown tabby cats.

At Price Road, Mother and Dad come into my room. We go out for breakfast to a country inn. I am sitting next to Jerry Wallace, typing at a desk. He says: "We are all in this together."

Looking in the mirror. Two faces, then I got it together and felt powerful and was looking at Ian. Made it with Alan. A sunny room. I can't find my watch.

So where are we on this novel? The wind rising, the leaves blowing away. And Kim is blowing away. Reading about a flood when here is a newscast of helicopter crashing into the Hudson because of the thunderstorm. It was named the *Mickey Mouse*. The helicopter was hit by lightning. All this in my book, accompanied by a tidal wave that wiped out a town. In *The Jonah* by David Herbert.

Dream of a place like the Resort in the Stiem book. A strange empty gray area. I was a fugitive and had the .22 Derringer. A party of a sort and I was introduced to a very tall, pale blond man who looked like Talbot and I told him so and it didn't mean anything. The Clifford person was showing me around. My status was highly ambiguous. Then the classic Ian dream and I am jealous and enraged by his neglect. Rage very real. Hell hath no fury like anybody scorned. I was saying goodbye and I was going somewhere and would never see him again. Alan or his equivalent was there as usual. I wanted him to feel my anger and he hardly noticed. And I thought I would go to Australia and get rich then he would be sorry but I knew there was no place to go, crossing a dark gray street. He has to be blind. Hmmmmmm. The man has to be blind. Hmmmmmm. Eye trouble. Hmmmmmm. I don't remember. Surround your Royal Wedding are DEAD Mick screams. Wrong party. Eternal BULLSHIT. Want a new car. His HIM and shot Mike in the poison flowers. Your tricks is finished as a film of the Royal Wedding. The sky rips paper room the empty room. We are inhuman voices from a star tornado sky. The sky rips starts to buckle and the eternal wind paper moon the empty room. Don't you realize . . .

Fliday. Imagine the journalist Bruce Elder asking if there was anything in my life I regret? *Madre de Dios!* There are mistakes too monstrous for remorse to tamper or to dally with! Remember the day Joan was killed and I was walking down the street and suddenly there were tears streaming down my face. When that happens, be careful. I have Billy's notes, bit and pieces here. Shuffle of photos in my mind. Billy in the taxi when I took him and left him with the maid in Mexico. Ian in Tangier there by the trees full of twittering sparrows. "Make it with me!"

"I remember shortly after my mother's death I was shuttled from place to place. In one of those places I was tucked in with all the amenities in a nice cozy room and cot. I don't know what time it was. I woke up and in an easy chair just across from my bed there sat a man. I couldn't make out his facial features because the room was dark. But he was dressed in a tasteful black suit and had his legs crossed, against which rested a cane. He was staring right at me. I began to scream uncontrollably."

I was taking a course. The students were all in an elevator or plane, it seems. We arrive at the third floor and here are about twelve students. I am sitting opposite the instructor on the floor. I was very uncertain as to what I would say. Then suddenly the students and the instructor were gone and I was alone. I looked around for ways to get out. On the way to the room where the course was conducted, we passed through an area where there were about twenty women . . . whores, it looked like. Then I went down stairs and then tried to get back up. There was a narrow ledge on which were various bric-a-brac: a clock in a block of glass, Victorian paperweights, and such things. I managed to get by them but there was no one on the third floor. I thought: This is the old snipe hunt.

Back down to the whore area. I was looking for a way to get out. I finally found a window covered with cellophane and managed to get it open and escape. A woman followed me out and finally two fat men pinned me down to the ground. I realize before, someone asked if I could sleep here and I said no. I didn't have my medication. Afterwards I had some papers of H. Spilled water on one of the papers. Snipe hunt Harbor Beach. The women.

"You don't have your education yet."

Watching Alan and Ian at the next table, a small table for two. I feel this longing and sadness, at the same time a *petulant annoyance*. Well, nobody seems to have considered me at all. I don't have a chicken, but desire to be in the same bed with them, and we are in the hall. I can see the bed inside my room but they won't come in. Do they even see me? Come to think of it, they don't. There is never an interchange in recognition of my presence. They simply walk around me and never answer when I say: "Ian . . . it's Billy here." He says nothing. Alan seems to know I am here, in a nasty way. It's like I want to make it with both of them or the composite *thing* they are.

Ian speak. What do you want? Burroughs is tuned to hear. The waiting room. Old film. 4 Calle Larachi. Old unhappy far-off things and battles long ago. Why do you still hate me? Ummmmm you're impossible! Go on . . . Past . . . Past . . . Billy . . . I . . . grind . . . neck . . . Boulder at sunrise . . . .36-caliber pistol . . . It was me all the time of course . . . Cabell was me . . . the curse came from me . . . The Japanese film *Death by Hanging*, a waiting room that is never used, contains only a urinal . . . In former times the fear piss was collected and used for magical purposes . . . of course fear sperm is better and Death Sperm is the best sperm what can be

got. The room in the dream was cluttered with unused furniture
. . . moldy musty dirty . . . with some dishes in the sink that had
been there for months . . . years perhaps. And the bed was dirty,
the sheets stunk of unwashed flesh years ago. When you turned
back the sheet it billowed out . . . smell of incense in a cloud, from
closet long to quiet vowed, moldering her lusts and books among,
as when a queen long dead was young. Under the dirty sheet I have
my pants down, half a hard-on. Ian beside me, his shirt and ratty-
looking tie still on.

Another Ian dream. I have been sleeping in his flat in his bed and
he is coming back. I am getting all my gear ready to go but I hope
he will ask me to stay. At some point Ian comes back. The flat is
quite large and very dusty. I can see curls of dust on the floor. I
remember my body warmth in his bed.

Ian looking great in a blue shirt, his eyes a deep blue, almost violet, and the slight sarcastic smile, his face glowing with
health.

The same night Kim is steering an intricate craft of metal. Different levels of platforms and catwalks and ladders. Wind whistling
through the metal. Wasn't Ian leaning elegantly on one of the metal
shelves, and looking at him with the old mocking look?

"Billy, don't be silly."

Yesterday was thinking about my missed appointment with eye doctor when this eye test notice comes on the TV screen. Today as I
make my bed at 10:00 a.m., I am thinking that I am by and large
a very happy man. People and critics like to think of me in despair
because they hate to think of anyone whose way of life they dis-

approve of as being happy. So I open the scrapbook to page 20. Freud says that the only happy men are those whose boyhood dreams are realized. The danger is to walk through life without seeing anything. Last night more vivid withdrawal dreams. A woman judge, the same one as in the dream in *Port of Saints,* is deciding whether to hand down a jail sentence on my writing.

In an alien place . . . series of islands. I keep forgetting my cane since my feet have healed. When I first got here I could hardly walk. James, John, and myself set out to explore the city. I can see a spire of buildings and decide that the center of town must be in that direction. A lot of people, a plane without wings on display. These weapons are everywhere. A man with weapons in a little glass or plastic case attached just behind his ear. I am afraid of missing the boat.

"Do not corrupt Allah's will, dreading your actions done."

Withdrawal nightmares. Egyptian scene. We were to be burned to death. Taken to the burning place. I could see people tied to stakes. The officials were black, with white painted eyes and white tunics. We decide to commit suicide and I slice off someone's neck. I try to stab myself with an ice pick. We run down a long corridor like a basement or subway. There is a guard at the end. I grab a water glass and break it off. The guard is making gestures like you can't do this. I shove the glass in his face and he goes down. We run up a slope. It is half inside and half outside, like a ramp that goes through room or ship. Come to a table. James says: "I need shoes." Beckett is there. Now I start back with a boy. We are kissing in front of black glass door as I say: "Where shall we go?"

Ian and I at Scientology center. A lunch counter and a number of women lounging about like mannequins. Some dish on the menu, and I ask what it is. "Just tell me what it looks like."

"Well," says the petite blue-eyed blonde behind the counter, "it's banana chips fried in a cream sauce . . ."

And just down the counter is a liz, naked to the waist, eating a whole plateful of this muck. The whole set is garish, like a 1920 movie theater, with red marble columns and mirrors and marble staircases.

The boys set up a guerrilla unit with the young Maize God. Traveling in time on the sacred books, they pick up allies: Tío Mate, an old assassin with eight deer on his gun, followed by El Mono, his adolescent Ka. Wild boys with eighteen-inch Bowie knives, head hunters and bandits, Castro and Chinese guerrillas, Black Panthers and hippies.

The priests have not been idle. They have opened negotiations with the United Fruit Company to arrange for a landing of Marines. They send in an agent to infiltrate the guerrillas.

The agent shows up at a guerrilla encampment:

"Shucks fellers, you got a *reefer?*"

"Who is this mother?"

A Black Panther with a submachine gun and a headhunter with a spear cover the stranger.

"You here to report to the head shrinker for a security check?"

The Security Department is divided down the middle into two sets. On one side is a brisk Scientology auditor with an E Meter set up on a card table.

"Will you pick up the cans please. Thank you."

On the other side is a grass hut with shrunken heads on shelves.

The head hunter takes up a stand facing the agent with his spear raised. Seated on a high chair is a Death Dwarf with larval flesh and skeleton face. He reaches forward and takes the agent's other hand with dry electric fingers.

"Do you know any CIA men personally?"

The agent looks wildly around at the shrunken heads of his predecessors.

"That reads . . . What do you consider that could mean?"

"The whole idea is repugnant to me. I'd as soon make a friend of a cobra."

"LIE. LIE. LIE," screams the Death Dwarf.

"Why, I've always been a Commie."

"That reads . . . What do you consider this could mean?"

"LIE. LIE. LIE."

"Do you have any unkind thoughts about M.O.B.? . . . That reads . . . What do you consider this could mean?"

"Why, all I ever wanted to do was mind my own business and smoke *reefers*."

"There's another read here."

"LIE. LIE. LIE."

"Are you connected to the CIA? Are you a CIA agent?"

"You got me wrong. I swear to you on my Scout's honor . . ."

"LIE. LIE. LIE."

"That ROCKSLAMS. What do you consider this could mean?"

The agent's head shrinks to the size of a fist and takes its place on the shelf.

In bed with James. Slipped out onto the floor. Pajamas open, got a hard-on. Out in a barn, looked out through lattice doors and saw what looked like a puma but was a wolf. Checked shotgun to see if it was loaded. Both shells fired. Barnlike closet. Meet in closet bar in West Village. Michael pushed me out of bed. The Lemon Kid. As lemon dries in salt and air, I am freed from harm and all despair.

Landed on Planet Venus with John Brady. A tent city had been set up for the passengers. John was sleeping in the tent, I was outside looking at the night sky. Next morning John still sleeping. I walked around in tent city. The changes were difficult to pinpoint. Brion was holding court in a large tent, Felicity and others present. He discounted the idea that we were on Venus. Showed me a copy of the *Tribune* with a story about the two homosexual astronauts. Picture of them looked like two leather-faced old-time vaudeville hoofers. Names like Mitch Nichol and Harry Freeland. Harry had an act where he got himself up like the Statue of Liberty and Mitch got himself up in a buffalo suit to represent a nickel. Nichol and Free. There were pictures of both as children and young men. Felicity said Free looked cute as a little boy, at which time he already had his Statue of Liberty act going.

Later when they studied to be astronauts they teamed up and formed the double act. The story, which ran over several pages, told about how they were subject to a homosexual assault like in the movie at the Jewel. Outside I walked around and saw two metal objects that caught fire. "Stay away from those things!" I warned. Now flowers and bushes were catching fire and I said: "It is the burning bush."

I had left the camp and was talking to another group of passengers. I explained to them how a seemingly normal Earth scene had been transported to Venus. Pointed to a stretch of water.

I returned to find the first camp deserted and completely empty except for the empty tents. I sought him and found him not in the desolate markets. However my gear was on a bed: a heavy coat, toilet articles, change of clothes. I put on the clothes. Heavy clasp knife in pocket. Now some people had arrived at the gate. They greeted me as a leader, saying that they were all passengers on the Blink Ship. One, who was better-looking than the others, stroked my palm with a finger when we shook hands. Arab boy in the Socco Chico, a friend turned away never returns—you are very lucky if he does. I was lucky at this point.

With Alex Trocchi and Kafka. Kafka had cancer. We took a cab to the country club. Moroccan Ginger was the doorman and he said that Kafka could not come in. Inside, the members were eating at a cafeteria table. Walked around trying to find our way back out of the club. A sort of maze that ended up in a swimming pool and a Turkish bath. Finally found an exit and started down the road. Alex joined me with some firewood.

A place like a construction camp or a frontier settlement. Suggestion of bulldozers, Quonset huts, tent bars. I was carrying an old Colt Frontier .44 in my boot and then in my waistband, on my way to the cafeteria. Someone who looked like he stepped out of an old Western said to me: "One can exist here."

Billy as a child on top of a roof . . . a street between us . . . he is about to jump across. I see he can't make it and yell: "No! No!" A truck driven by my father, ninety miles per hour down a winding road. At one point in the camp a gray bird pecks at me furiously, screaming: *"Savage! Savage!"* He surveys the ruined Dike Fern. "Have got to get some bulldozers in here, Jody. Clean out all this crap."

Tent bars I was carrying down a winding road. Billy as a child in the camp, a gray cafeteria. Clean out this street between us.

A fight down by the edge of a dark lake, which shifted to a loft. The lock was faulty and I could not lock the door. I had a revolver. Now the door opened and someone was coming in. I wondered if it was death itself. John de C. came in and took the revolver. It was his set somehow.

After a party. People gone. Same loft. I walked down to the end of loft. Someone outside. I found a machete. In bathroom was a filing cabinet, a youth beside it. Tall and blond with "New York Work Room" printed on shirt. He was going through the filing cabinet. He looks like James, but is not quite James. Is this the boy from Middletown? He says something and smiles, indicating the filing cabinet.

Same loft. I was laughing and accused somehow of laughing at Mother. Fear in the dark room. I walk up towards the bed and James is sitting up in bed and I say: "If you turn back on self." He was a part of myself. Now there are people in the room, and a woman I recognize as an old enemy. I am in the bed and throw her a third-eye punch. She throws something back and we both laugh, but not in any friendly or conciliatory manner on either side . . . simply an open recognition of enmity.

In Clayton I start to walk out to Price Road, then decide it is too far. I turn back. Old barbed-wire entanglements around the town. I had been fighting the enemy as an underground agent years ago but my status was never recognized and I have been forgotten.

No hero's welcome. A Venusian woman involved. James and I in a dormitory. He is talking and I tell him finally that we should not talk because of other people trying to sleep.

A sort of amusement park with booths and exhibitions. I stop and order a sandwich, pointing to what I want. The counterman takes a bite out of the sandwich and drops it into a cup of some sort of gruel and hands it to me. I say: "You interplanetary Venusian son of a bitch!" and throw the cup at his head. He comes out from behind the counter. I tell him I am interplanetary, too, but not same planet. He is about to hit me, but tells me the Countess has intervened on my behalf. I will be taken to friends.

On bus waiting for my stop. Finally arrive at Dr. Bellows' clinic. Inside I am tortured . . . my hands broken. I say: "What is this for, friends?" and they say, "What did you expect?" I fight them off, then am threatened with the ovens.

There is a Lulow in the room (an animal like a possum, native to the area, depicted in Bosch). It snaps at my white tennis shoes. I seem to be able to escape.

A duel with pistols in which the contestants walked around a big square—one from one entrance and one from another. The square is like a market, like the Mercado Mayorista in Lima.

Ian is in one locality and I go beyond this area and then come back. He says he didn't want to keep me in his area because "there is nothing very interesting on campus." Then at six o'clock we go down to the Campus Bar where a number of people are already assembled.

A scorpion fish. I was in a pension and I saw two scorpions on the wall with long tails.

In Greece with Gregory, looking very smart in sports jacket and slacks and in good health. Self-confident and well dressed. He says: "Well, you were self-contained but not self-confident and now you are self-confident but not self-contained." I am buying laudanum, which seems to be more or less legal.

In Athens with Chester Kallman and Alan Ansen. In a hotel room on the thirteenth floor. There is one of those windows that fold halfway and I say: "Of course I could jump out the window and float down." I demonstrate levitation in the room, floating a few feet above the floor—standing and lying down. An argument with Chester, who thinks the police would stop the drug traffic if they could. I am for some reason very angry and call him an idiot for thinking they really want to do this.

A lot of this spilling over into *Ticket That Exploded, The Soft Machine,* and especially *Nova Express.* It reads thin now—dim and grainy—an old film.

So here I am in Lawrence, Kansas, the *Day After* town.

TV commercial:
When your hemorrhoids flare up
Fight fire with TUCK
Soothes on contact.
Suppose we got no soothing tuck
What the fuck?
In any store
What store?
Brothers, your hemorrhoids flare up
Nobody gives a flying fuck
Got more pressing things in mind
Like being stone blind

Blind from the light and the heat
Lucky ones is just charred meat.

Fletch slept on my bed. Dreams about him. He is outside a carved gate of metal screening. I save him from falling off a thousand-foot drop. I am very sick without methadone. I need a tablet before breakfast.

Quarreled with Allen Ginsberg. We are not on speaking terms. Don't know why.

I was looking for library in Paris or was it Moscow? We passed a huge building occupying an entire block. Through the windows I could see stacks and people reading.

Turning to the left down a side street, we came to a special library more suited to our purposes. A man dressed like a priest was the receptionist.

I took off my cap and after waiting a short time with some other people who wanted to use the library I went in and found it was more a museum than a library. Very much like the museum in *The Place of Dead Roads*.

I found several coins, one a quarter with an Indian head which was, it seemed, quite valuable.

I was wearing a lumpy brown suit with a stain. Dark stain on a lump of the cloth.

A packing dream. This time it wasn't that there was more gear than could fit into the suitcase I have. It's that I can't find my suitcase at all. Finally I find three old beat-up, dented suitcases, like the abandoned cases out in the garage. Can I even use them at all? Ian seems to be present in a different, helpful role. He has changed roles since the Cat Revelation. Since the White Cat. This was a basic turning point. Do not remember where I was going in the dream. Just preoccupied with the suitcases. I knew it would take me at least half an hour to pack, and there was not much time, as always in these packing dreams.

Professional gun people are a real race apart. I mean gun writers and contestants. Actually they can make a fair living. But it certainly is hermetic, like ballet dancers. They can't think or talk about anything else. Here are some of Skeeter's boring memories: "Over drinks, the cops talked shop. Cattle rustling was generally condemned. Then the talk, as it always does among men like these, turned to guns."

Something creepy about it. "All right, boys, let's cut the horseshit and get down to what it is all about." There's something, well—diseased about it. A hundred years ago, of course, there was real danger, and real need for guns. All right, many of them are or were lawmen. More were than are, not talking about that, talking about the mainstream. But now it can get like a bell jar full of precious Lesbians. Different content—same hermetic recycling atmosphere. Suffocating. A little backwater.

Remember a TV picture of a ghost town—Bradshaw, Texas. A real ghost town. Gray and grainy. Some old gunfighter in a rocking chair. You can see right through him to the dusty sagebrush. All these gun world characters like Elmer Keith. Must read his book: *Hell, I Was There.* Some of them seem dedicated to idiotic self-glorification and pontifical statements on the relative merits of .45 and 9-millimeter calibers.

It's a dead world. Peopled by folkloric ghosts. There have been no basic changes in small arms since the self-contained cartridge and the semiauto design of 1911. Nobody has eliminated the basic flaw of the revolver: gap between cylinder and barrel. Or the differential pressure of a spring magazine. So what are you getting down to, Skeeter?

This is Thor's day, and Thor is the God of Firearms. He could throw an energy blast from his hammer would level a Western set. A bolt of energy. Now it is all done by a contrivance. Hell, I was there. But I didn't stay there. A veteran of many viruses. One of the few to survive the Hanging Fever. After that, the Gun Sickness was easy and greasy. Meooooow. Now the cat virus threatens to smother me in cats . . .

I was talking with a rich boy in what looked like a truck. He asked if I wouldn't like to live completely without problems, say in Greece maybe, nice climate, everything provided? I say: "When we find out what we are actually doing and who we actually are, that is the point of living . . . it may be only a few seconds . . . a few seconds of significant action, out of a lifetime . . ."

By now I find out he has no money, having frittered his money away.

"In obviously unwise investments," I put in. "Yes, well he's got nothing now, so his offer is invalid in any case." We start to make it but he is very unattractive, covered with a black fuzz from head to foot, and his penis is diseased or deformed, like old rotten wood or porous stone, full of fissures and perforations.

His name, it seems, is Allen.

Iwas sleeping in a room where the furniture was covered with drapes. A musty smell of disuse. There was someone else there who was sleeping under a drape over the bed, as I was myself. A little black dog came into the room. It was squirming and wagging its tail. I picked it up by the back and it tried to bite, and I pried its mouth open holding the jaws.

A phantom black dog, like a banshee, is a harbinger of death. *The Unbearable Bassington:* "A small black dog followed him into the dining room. He died shortly afterwards in Africa." I recall the horrible little black stray dog that ruined Snap, our Irish terrier. We were supposed to get pure-blooded Irish puppies and instead there was a litter of black mongrels, and Snap died as a result of the pregnancy. She was buried behind the garden, and later when I was digging out a fish pool I came upon her bones.

Whose death? I do not like it. I can feel death.

So just as the cats represent various figures from my past, the same applies to daytime people. Wayne Propst is always the one you wake up to. *Where am I??!!* And the first face you see is Wayne Propst. So Wayne is the face you come to as you wake up . . .

Who could have observed and created a centipede? I see a centipede, about three feet long, coming into the room. It rubs against the doorjamb like a cat and spreads its pincers and makes an indescribable sound of insect ingratiation.

The .38 slumped from my hand into my lap. The centipede was of a bright red and translucent. My God, I am about to pet a centipede! I petted it. It turned around and went away through an invisible diaphragm.

All abilities are paid for with disabilities. Perfect health may entail the heavy toll of bovine stupidity. Insight in one area involves blind spots in another. I could not have done what I have done as a writer had I been a gifted mathematician or physicist.

Honesty wrung out of him by pain, he cried out with a loud voice.

Go into a restaurant to call a Mr. Shawn on the phone to buy coke. Don't know why, since I don't like it. I am with Cabell Hardy and can see into his mind confusion. I can overhear a table of people fifty feet away saying that we are lovers. No anger involved. Gothenberg, Sweden—remember? Well, randomize is the answer to continuing computerized phantom insulters and remember that one of the first cutups took place at the University of Gothenberg. So that is your answer: Randomize the program of the computer and you reduce and neutralize the effect. Here the table is not threatening. I have put it out in the street.

On a train going to Switzerland with Mikey Portman and Alan Watson. Interviewed by a reporter. I point out that he is missing the story. Story that I am a writer as well known as Graham Greene.

"And I have a restaurant."

Calico and Fletch are sleeping on my bed. Dream they are under the covers by my feet and then rushing around the room. I see a feather. (This morning Wimpy brought a dead bird into the house.) Then I find on a shelf a large mouse of strange gray-green color like plasticine. The mouse turns into a revolver. Then I find that there is pus on my hands and wrist. Gobs of yellow pus.

My analysis. Many years, a lot of money—one would be tempted to say complete waste of time and money, but no experience is ever lost on a writer. I would prefer not to discuss my horrible old condition at the beginning of a long period of analyses and psychotherapy, but on the other hand, I could get around, hold down jobs. Well, something happened and some little key was turned . . . perhaps so that I went on to do what I have done. Maybe no connection. It's like the one percent of penicillin in old Chinese prescriptions. They didn't know what the one percent was or more accurately *where*. And my gut feeling is that all there was in all this is a couch. This is the reason I am not buying a new couch, to save money. Anyhoo. There was a time . . . oh well . . . Dr. Federn, who killed himself. Nice old gentleman.

Did I seriously consider this any proof of telepathy?

I replied: "My dear shrink, I do not consider anything proof of anything, in any case, not involved in proving anything."

Like a young thief thinks he has a license to steal, a young writer thinks he has a license to write. You know what I mean right enough: riding along on it, it's coming faster than you can get it down and you know it's the real thing, you can't fake it, the writer has to have *been* there and make it back. Then it hits you, cold and heavy, like a cop's blackjack on a winter night: *Writer's Block*. Oh yes, he tried to warn me, the old hand, "You write too much, Bill . . ." I wouldn't listen.

Then it slugs you in the guts. For a whole year I couldn't remember my dreams. Tried going without pot and everything. It was like some gray bureaucrat wiped away the dream before my eyes as I tried to grasp one detail that would bring the dream back, the outlines: dead. James complained I sat for hours in my chair at the end of the loft, doing absolutely nothing. Stagnating without tranquillity. The pages and pages with nothing in them: the writer has been nowhere and brought nothing back. The false starts, the brief enthusiasm. Books that died for the lack of any reason to stay alive after ten pages.

Then you get it back. It's there. You know. You can feel it, like the opening character . . . I was there on that mesa with Kim. Kim, my spacecraft for travels in the nineteenth century. I could see it from where I was, the arrowhead there in my hand. The dizzy awe, as if you could flash back through the millions or so years to the beginning, the caves, the hunger. Kim knew he had always been gay, making sex magic in front of the paintings to activate them, covered with animal skins he whines and growls and whimpers off, his sperm drips down the animals' flanks. Kim adored these animal impersonations. He was turning into the animals and found he had much more in common with the predators than the herbivores. You can see what a dog or a cat is thinking, but the mind of a deer is a strange place, a strange green place. It's hard to get in there. The men swaying about with antlers on their heads are trying to get into it, mindless and beautiful.

Don't want to write this. Have said no honest autobiography has ever been attempted, much less written, and no one could bear to read it. At this point I guess the reader thinks I am about to confess some juicy sex practices. Hardly. Guess I was twenty-four, working in the shop at Cobble Stone Gardens, which I hate to remember, when this Jew woman sent me around to the servants' entrance and I drove away clashing the gears and saying: "*Hitler is perfectly right!*" So you want it honest? You vant? You vant? You vant?

One afternoon, Kramer was there, and you could say about him, as Toots Shor said about Jimmy Walker at Walker's coffin: "Jimmy, when you walked in you brightened up the joint."

And I said: "Since I've had this job, my voice is changing."

And Dave says something about "the Catlins, you know them."

"I'm acquainted with the family," I said in my obsequious manner, and we had a laugh.

Stalling. Don't want to go on.

This context, one night in the house at Price Road. Went down to the icebox. (I was wretchedly unhappy. No sex. No work that meant anything—nothing.) Dad was there eating something. It's a suburban custom, raiding the icebox. "Hello, Bill." It was a little-boy voice pleading for love, and I looked at him with cold hate. I could see him wither under my eyes as I muttered, "Hello."

Looking back now, I feel an ache in the chest where the Ba lives. I reach out to him: *Dad! Dad! Dad!*

Too late. Over from Cobble Stone Gardens.

When Mother was in Chastains Nursing Home in St. Louis the last four years of her life, I never went to see her. Just sent mawkish cards from London on Mother's Day, and occasionally postcards from here and there. Remember years ago—fifty? don't remember —she once said to me: "Suppose I was very sick. Would you come to see me? Look after me? Care for me? I'm counting on that being true."

It wasn't. The telegram from Mort. I had been gotten out of bed. For a moment I put this aside. "Mother dead." No feeling at all. Then it hit, like a kick in the stomach.

I was in Tangier. Before dinner, which was to be in a large dining hall. Steaks were sizzling on the griddle offstage. I decided to have a cocktail before dinner, and went to the bar. The bartender informs me that no mixed drinks can be served. In a dusty case I can see a pint of gin and a fifth of some dubious Scotch. No, I cannot buy a bottle, because the hours are not right. It looks like at least half an hour until dinner, so I set out for the Parade Bar.

Come to an apartment house and get in an elevator that takes me to the top floor. This seems to be the bedroom of a mulatto. The bar is on the third floor. Disembarking on the third floor, I find out that no drinks can be served here either. It is a new law. Back in the dining room I find out that no bars are left in Tangier, owing to strict new laws passed by the orthodox Muslim governor. No alcohol may be consumed in Tangier and that's it. However, someone hands me a paper cup of straight gin, which I drink. Maybe there will be some rotgut Moroccan wine with dinner, but this is doubtful.

I am walking up a slope thinking I will feel very good in the morning, no alcohol at all. Reminded of Kells in Corfu, walking up a slope and suddenly he is sweating and on the verge of collapse. He told me this in Tangier, and added: "I know you are dead and I think I am dead too." So in this dream I am in the Land of the Dead. After reading Brion's Bardo Museum book, so it is not surprising that no alcohol is allowed. The steaks will be ready in a very few minutes. The Parade Bar. Well, Jay Hazelwood dropped dead there of a heart attack.

There was another installment to the dream which I forget. Well, I am slipping into Brion's style. Out front the yard is full of branches broken off by the ice. Remember the ice storm when I was a child. We had no power for two weeks at Christmastime. Had to burn wood in the oil burner. Then the power is back on, and my little electric steam engine is hissing away and smelling cleanly of oil.

That black boy did a very sloppy job of mowing the lawn. Insolent sloppiness. Insolence in every corner where he didn't go back to finish, insolence in the grass left on the walkway, insolence in the wide margin given the flowers. "Sure Whitey, I'll be careful of your fucking flowers." So I hand him the ten. He takes it and looks at it and puts it in his pocket and walks away without a word. WELL, no more of the Clark brothers here. I don't like their sullen insulting faces.

My father in a swimming pool. Went down and came up.

The Italian lady. I say: "I do not intend to marry," and she says: "You are rather too much for the field."

The Devil's Bargain applied to a country. If ever a country had the potential to escape the bargain and really fulfill the promises, it was America.

And what happened?

"Sell me the American Dream, the American Soul, and I will give you refrigerators groaning with Malvern Spring Water and venison sausage. I will give you remote-controlled color television. I will give you two cars in every garage."

(At the expense of people starving in remote unimportant Third World areas.)

"You agree?"

An idiot chorus: *"Yes Yes Yes."*

"And I will give you the POWER to keep what you have."

Hiroshima.

Sure, we were the only ones that had it then. There were those who said we should have gone and followed through and taken out the Rooskis and the Chinese and ruled the fucking world. Little men. Fumbled the big ball—*Thank God.*

Sek is oil. That the Duad stinks of burning synthetics is only natural, coal tar products squirted out of the transmutations of mineral shit, squirted out at tremendous pressure, released by the enema drills. Burning plastic is an ancient stink . . . so is rotting oranges. Anita Bryant, clean taste of orange juice in a hundred million throats, the dazzling teeth, the sweet orange breath. All too sour and putrid, rot behind the Tampax and deodorants.

Here is Daisy, a habit-forming deodorant that is injected in the vein. When you got Daisy, you smell like fresh-cut grass, flowers, ozone, sea spray . . . everything *clean*. And boy, when your Daisy runs out, how you stink. And it takes more and more Daisy just to keep your smell on an even keel.

You can run out in a crowded street or in a supermarket:

"My God, what's that stink?"

It narrows down . . .

"It's him . . . It's her . . ."

"Now look, you have to get out of here."

"Let's get the filthy bastard."

He makes a run for the toilet and comes out smelling like water hyacinths.

"I think there has been a mistake here."

Better get home fast, Mr. Daisy junky.

Ian and the Stones. Vague resentment. A performance. I was dressed in some outlandish eighteenth-century costume. But I was not slated to perform, just to be there, which I resented. Savoy book and the Ritz performance. "Performance." Mick Jagger and Nic Roeg. "The Cut-Ups." Antony Balch. Eclipse, a dimness like underexposure.

"These cold and tangled streets that once were gay with light and drink, now echo to my tread as I pass by alone. Night breezes

thread through dusty rooms and carry out through broken win-
dowpanes old thoughts and memories. The lad is far away who
cherished these, and nothing of his spirit now remains." (Colin
LePauvre)

A feeling of universal damage and loss. Ginger wanders about
the house and the back lot, moaning for her lost kittens. She jumps
into my lap and nuzzles at me. The eclipse seems to be over, and
the light slowly comes on. The sky darkens and goes out, and leave
the details to Joe.

Brion on set. We were all housed in a *pension* with large bare
rooms, like St. Martin's in Cambridge, or was it St. Mary's, where
I stayed for a week when Ian was in Cambridge and rented a large
room overlooking the market. It contained a sofa and one narrow
bed, and the landlady was always snuffling around when we made
it, so one could never relax.

Looking out over this market, I got the idea of color separation.
Look out there and pick out all the reds; now all the blues; now
the green shutters on the stalls, and trees, and a sign; the yellows,
a truck, a license plate, a fire hydrant; the reds, a stop sign, a
sweater, some flowers; the blues the sky a coat, a sign on the side
of a truck . . . later elaborated into the "color walk." I recall the
feeling of strain, of not quite being able to do it.

Exercises like that don't break the chains of association. All they
do is delineate and define the bars, let you know they are there,
and that is already a lot. A man who doesn't know he is in prison
can never escape. As soon as you realize the planet and your body
constitute an almost escape-proof jail—yellow, a truck, a fire hydrant, flowers out the window; red car goes by, a little boy with red
shirt and cap walks by, now another big red panel-truck turns onto
Nineteenth Street—as soon as you know you are in prison, you have
a possibility to escape.

What is old Mrs. Hemphill burning in her driveway? Old love

letters, perhaps, raking at a small fire . . . a clear crime against fire regulations right there, perhaps I should turn her in to the Fire Department or make a citizen's arrest—a yellow car, a pale blue car, there is another blue car, brighter blue, right on cue, another shift to yellow—white—beige—no good *no bueno*—now yellow, now red, now a yellow truck.

June 3 is Ian's birthday and it is not surprising that I had a long typical dream about him Sunday night. It would indeed have been surprising if I had not dreamed of such a persistent dreamboat. Let's see, Ian would have been forty-three, or is it forty-four?

So for the June 3 dream, we are on a large boat. Now, Ian and Alan Watson are there, and we are invited to the house of a queer white slaver. Some reference to a Chinese restaurant. I am talking to Alan about immortality.

"Just who," I inquire provocatively, "is immortal? Is it you, or some other instance that looks like you?"

And last night we are on this boat. I ask James:

"Aren't we paying for Ian to stay here a week?"

James says, "Yes."

"Well," I demand, "where the fuck is he?"

In fact, I haven't seen him since his arrival, and then he was very hostile. What is this? I am soaring out over a complex of futuristic buildings, so strange-looking I cannot be sure of their function. Now I am back on the boat, and Ian stands smiling behind a bar. He is wearing a white shirt with no tie, open at the neck, and looks quite young.

A restaurant in Alaska. I am with someone I intended to kill, for no reason that I can remember. Alaska has an area set aside for the concentration of dissidents. The restaurant is huge, with fifty-foot ceilings, smoky, and half underground at the sides. Light comes in from windows between pillars. There are long tables with thick bread, bacon and eggs.

I like it. We are going out again, and I am putting on rubbers like women's, with high heels. They don't seem to fit.

People who grow their own meat on their own bodies . . . like arm bacon and leg roasts. It grows back, but not quick enough to keep up, so that they are always in danger of eating themselves. In fact, so delectable is the flavor of liver, they can hardly restrain themselves from cutting their bodies open and eating it, although they know this is fatal. However, the recuperative growth is amazing. If, say, they only eat half the liver, they can make it. And some have been known to eat their hearts out, and die in gastronomic ecstasies. The brain is especially toothsome, and it is an awesome sight to see a self-eater dipping into a hole on top of his skull and eating the raw brain, with an expression of ever-increasing idiot relish.

For some reason I had a bad feeling about the shooting expedition. Out to Gary Palka's place, to shoot into a bale of hay as a backstop. Bill Rich, Anne Wattlings, and your reporter and Andrew Wadsworth, an apostate Psychic Youth from kinky England. We were cut off by another car turning in to a gas station, and by a Japanese woman in another car, and I thought, These are bad omens.

We go into Ludwig's gun shop, and his handsome son sold me some .38 special reloads in a plastic sack for $7.50 and some .45 hardballs for $13. We get out to shoot, and I load up the Ruger with these .38 reloads and the cylinder won't turn. Projecting primer. Had to take the cylinder out to get the bad case out. And this happened again. Then a misfire. Then a strange little pop. But we recovered an *empty case.* Nobody is hitting shit, and my guardian angel tells me to pack it in. On the way back two more cutoffs, one turning in to Dillons.

This morning when I go to clean the gun, the rod won't go through. I push as hard as I can . . . still no go, so I get the heaviest rod and pound it with the cylinder and a bullet comes out that was lodged in the barrel about two inches from the breech. Obviously the cartridge had no powder, just the primer. Just enough to wedge it firmly in the barrel. So I may well owe my hand to my Khu. The Khu was telling me: *Boxed in. Boxed in. Wrap it up.* We had only fired a few shots, but I just suddenly decided *no more for today.*

Well, why not. That was then and this is now. Used to be a thief myself, now I am down heavy on burglars. Taking what a man makes honest. There is something basically wrong about a thief, and the whole spiritual concept of theft. For the magic world runs on theft. You don't create magic, you steal it. Hmmmmmm. I will say that anything that is truly mine cannot be stolen. Which is a lot of bullshit, of course. You can tell when some old wise guy is going to shit out some wisdom on you. "My son, what is truly yours will always be yours. And I will always be with you." Uh . . . Nice old vampire. Take a little, leave a little, so where can a man find the truth? The truth is in front of him, below him, above him, and to all sides. Tiny slices of truth that overlap, tear each other to pieces, what does it matter. The only thing that matters is your perception of truth. Not so hard.

Good and evil? Well, any uncorrupted intelligence knows a prick when he sees one. Reading you the rules, and very glad he can't do anything for you. And the man who helps for no particular reason . . . *"Farmacía"* . . . Nice guys and shits. And who has never said,

"What a nice place this planet could be to live on if all the shits was flushed down the drain." All these shits telling us what we are going to eat and drink, shoot, sniff or shove up your ass. It's my own business.

"What are you doing in there, Mr. Reagan?" An alert narcotics officer has apprehended the Chief Executive sticking an opium suppository up his ass.

"I won by a hemorrhoid," the agent confessed.

Another half second and it would have been shoved up into the amendment about you can't be required to testify against yourself nor can your vomit or shit be so called to testify.

W here the servant is led beyond his depth by the master, who intends—or at least believes he intends—to help the servant and lead him to the Western Lands. Then he sees it just isn't going to work. It's heartbreaking, and also very dangerous. Because the servant *knows*. A blast of hate from the heavy heart of an old servant.

Old unhappy far-off things stirred up as I edit, as if I didn't have enough unhappy things right here, right now.

May Day May Day May Day
 Back to April Don't like May
But why . . . instance . . . Let the subconscious run riot. It will reveal all, as Kerouac used to say—still think so, Jack? I still hold that trust fund against you, the Russian countess is no trouble. April is the cruelest month, stirring dull roots with spring rain, mixing memory and desire . . . knowing laugh of the dead. Oh yes, that was an arbitrary backdate about the cat. Am I putting the cat out of time, just as I bar it out of the house?

Of course, the same considerations about cats apply to people . . . It happens I pick up someone like John Brady or John Culverwell and postulate some complex psychic relationship, which is partly valid enough, so like the cat they have had a glimpse, and they are much worse off than before, would have been much better off never to have met me.

Truth be told, that can be said of quite a few people. Writers do tend to be bad luck. No trouble . . . no story.

L. Ron Hubbard, the founder of Scientology, says that the secret of life has at last been discovered—by *him*. The secret of life is *to survive*. The rightest right a man could be would be to live infinitely long. And I venture to suggest that the wrongest wrong a man could be might well be the means whereby such relative immortality was obtained. To survive what, exactly? Enemy attack, what else?

We have now come full circle, from nineteenth-century crude literalism through behaviorism, the conditioned reflex, back to the magical universe, where nothing happens unless some force, being, or power wills it to happen. He was killed by a snake? Who murdered him? He dies of a fever? Who put the fever curse on him?

It's 5:02 p.m., Monday, August 6, Hiroshima Day. I have been thinking all afternoon about a silly old song, 1948 or earlier:

Bongobongobongo
I'm so happy in the Congo

Got this book I picked up in Dillons this afternoon, called *Metzger's Dog,* won out in a coin toss over *Realm Seven.* (Take a book, any book.) Page 16: "Immelmann began to glare at him, so Chinese Gordon shifted to 'Bongo Bongo Bongo, I Don't Want to Leave the Congo.'"

Coincidence, say the anti-ESPs. Doesn't mean a thing.

It was a Monday. In the future city from *Blade Runner.* I am in my room at Price Road, in the bed. Allen Ginsberg is there, much slimmer and clean-shaven, and a slender young man with sandy hair and sharp features. I can't see his clothes, seems to be in a brocaded jacket. He says: "I am the other half of William Burroughs." Familiar as myself, but I can't quite place him. It isn't exactly Ian. He walks away and I follow him, into the city. There are some androids in a square, and he goes away with an android before I can question him further.

There is a doctor, with a gray mustache and a gray suit and silver-rimmed glasses, who takes a look at my foot, pulling out a long thread, like catgut, and someone says: "They can do something now." I keep looking for the Other Half Boy. Who is he, exactly? That is exactly the point. He isn't anyone exactly.

A slender young man with sandy hair and rather sharp features refers to *The Gates of Anubis,* which takes place in early eighteenth-century England. A girl who pretends to be a boy is a key figure, and there are some good bits. The Gates of Anubis lead to the Land of the Dead. I think the reference here is to some Egyptian incestuous relationship with my dark sister.

I have a twitch in the flesh of my calves. Little seismic tremors, quite impossible to control, as if there was something just under the skin continually moving with autonomous life. Dr. Gray says it is the residue of a virus attack, a neural pattern that is functioning on its own, like some remote, uncontrollable segment of a computer.

I was giving birth to a child in a Land of the Dead *pension*. Someone has tried to kill me. Will it be in the papers? Seems not, because no reporters have come to interview me.

Marmalade all over my walking stick . . .

Dream long enough and dream hard enough
    You will come to know
    Dreaming can make it so . . .

But they are cutting off our dreams—dreams don't mean much, they say, and proceed to make it so. Night after night, with no dreams I can remember. Anatole Broyard said: "Shall WE continue to inspire books like *The Place of Dead Roads?*" I can feel the Wiper wipe away the dream traces . . . fading like steps in wind-blown sand or snow. Wipe. Wipe. The road to the Western Lands is still open. Just step back. Cut reaction lines. With an obsidian knife. The Western Lands . . . a floating feeling, absence of fear . . . nothing between you and what you see . . . vacant lots, a crumbling brick wall . . . weeds . . . a fence, a field beyond . . . moving drifting drifting a muddy river, brown water pouring through a logjam, weeds and grass . . . a glade, the little green reindeer.

⚊ ⚊ ⚊

In a restaurant, and Stewart Gordon is there in a black coat, with his horrible knowing smirk. We are sitting at a table and he overturns a glass of lemonade and vodka on the table and I am about to give him a real piece of my mind for being an all-around nuisance.

Walking out of the bar and down through an underpass. Here I meet several people who are friendly, in an ambiguous fashion. There is a short, slender old man with a white beard. And a young man, his face pale and smooth as ivory, looking something like Chris Lucas; he has sharp Gothic features and is carrying a swagger stick. There is a third man present, but I draw a blank on his appearance. Who is the third?

I go down a flight of stairs and a yellow dog follows me. The dog has a very sharp muzzle that comes to a point, almost like the point on the end of a trail blazer, an all-around weapon. You unscrew the compass which serves as the knob of the cane, and there is a sharp machine-turned point, so you can use the weapon as a lance or a push dagger. Well, why not just carry a heavy cane and a knife? This is a curious dog, with its pointed head, seems friendly or at least not overtly hostile.

"Aren't we paying for Ian to stay here a week? Well, where the fuck is he?"

Back on the boat and he stands behind the bar, smiling. A creature like a goat or a chamois comes out from under the waterlogged house . . . a restaurant in Alaska with fifty-foot ceiling, smoky and half underground . . . Alan Watson says to me: "There is something wrong with your eyes."

In the pension. I had two keys, one with an ordinary tab. Was I supposed to leave it at the desk? The other was a key on a large metal ring. This was for another room I had reserved but not used, and I am worried that I will have to pay for this room and that I should tell them I am not going to use it and turn my key in.

Ian is there and seems quite different. Respectful. He says he is reconstituting the various meetings we had and the places where the meetings took place. He will visit the locations wherever possible. We are in a town like New Orleans. Phone call from Jay Friedheim from New Orleans this morning. My room is a mess. The bed unmade is a tangle of comforters and blankets. Pink blankets. Ian has a room adjoining mine.

It's like a typewriter attached to your throat, all the time draining it out of you, you gotta have it, and it is taking more and more . . . *Clinic* . . . *Clinic* . . . *Clinic* . . .

So, Anatole Broyard, you wish to contact me? I think I have half a page for the message.

Please, please, Mr. Burroughs.

Go on, please.

I am told what I will write.

I understand perfectly. Sources?

Don't know. Voices in my head.

Ever try disobeying?

Yes. Results were horrific, headaches and bad luck. Can you help me, Burroughs?

I don't know. I will do what I can.

There was something very disquieting in the fact that the man showed no reaction. The doctor had expected him to renew his pleas, stand up, even offer violence. (The doctor was a black-belt karate man and he had nothing to fear from this elderly man.) The man just sat there, his face empty of expression, his face empty as an empty mirror.

"I have said I have to go, and I am locking up the office."

The man nodded, without moving.

Oh God, do I have to throw him out?

"I have no objection to your going. As soon as you give me the Rx."

"Look, I've told you, I'm not going to give you a prescription for narcotics. Now be thankful I don't call the police, and get out!"

The doctor became aware that the man had repeated his words just behind him so that he stumbled on "get out . . . get towt . . ." It sounded grotesque.

The man smiled. "You are a ventriloquist, Doctor? You do imitations?"

The doctor took a deep breath.

"Get out of my office!"

The man walked to the door. Opened it.

"Weren't you going too, Doctor?"

Suddenly the doctor's control snapped. He stepped forward and hit the man in the jaw. The man fell like a mannequin. The doctor examined him quickly.

My God!

The man was dead.

Death in a dream is always equivocal. I have often tried to kill myself in a dream to avoid capture by police but I never seem to be really *dead*. The dream gets dimmer as I look. Some person is deliberately wiping away the traces. Seems that where he she it comes from one doesn't dream, or if one does one doesn't talk about it or even admit it, like the Victorian matron. "But we don't talk about the plumbing." A faint cold disapproval drifts from Ian's room at Egerton Gardens, where I stayed years ago after the first apomorphine cure with Dr. Dent.

My adolescent Ka came to my room, which was on the second floor overlooking a back garden. I said, "You don't seem glad to see me," and he said, "I hate you." And who could blame him for that? These meetings are usually catastrophic. It is normal. What could I say . . . Been out here with the animals of the village . . . you don't know what it's like here. Day after day, tomorrow and tomorrow . . . it wears you down. So stop complaining and you may find out what you are complaining about. So? The silences. The absence.

Generally speaking, in a ghost town you can see what gave out . . . the gold, the oil, the diamonds. But on this nameless island even the ghost is gone. On the highest point of the island, some fifteen hundred feet above the bay and the rotting pier, stands an enigmatic office building, some twelve stories high. The elevator can still be operated by a complex arrangement of pulleys and levers, if there is someone there to operate it. The only one left is the Consul. From this Consul of some unspecified locality, I must obtain a permission to sail a small boat from the island to San Francisco.

I already have the permission, an impressive document with red seals on heavy parchment, in a number of languages, living and dead. As soon as the boat itself arrives, I can proceed on my dubious journey across the Pacific at least. Meanwhile, the Consul has billeted me on the twelfth floor. Below me, empty offices with enigmatic gold lettering on glass doors . . . "Q.E.S. Developmental Limited," "P.S. Fach," "Mineral Perritos."

A large bare octagonal room. On one side a precarious balcony juts into space. The Consul ventures onto this balcony, where I hesitate to follow, and the wind blows his glasses off, spinning and glittering away in the afternoon sun.

At one time a sort of ski lift gave access to and from the waterfront, where a pier extends a hundred feet into the bay. Now the lift is overgrown with vines, and the mechanism caked with rust. No matter: a foot trail exists. The Consul tells me that no one stays on the waterfront, owing to the unbearable stagnant heat and a species of highly venomous flying scorpion.

"Even the toothpaste has gone bad. It's as bad as that."

"How can toothpaste go bad?"

"It can in Russia. It is normal."

She smiled all her teeth at me. It was unnerving. It was a powerful sight.

"If I smile, it means we are under surveillance. If I frown it is, how you say, OK."

"I smell a capybara. It is the largest of all rodents," he said tonelessly.

"How can you be sure?"

"In Russia everything is sure. In the West, nothing. That is the difference."

"When the toothpaste goes bad, then nothing is lost."

"We have a saying that the teeth know more than the ass."

"Of course. They are there first."

"And when nothing is last, everything is first. It is normal."

"*Glasnost:* when everything is permitted and nothing is available."

"The age of information, when only informers are swell informed."

"You mean well informed."

"No. I mean swell informed. Swollen with information, like a bursting bladder."

"Or a cow needing to be milked."

"So long as there are milkers, there will be cows."

"Even when there is no more milk."

"Shall . . . with a monarch's voice cry havoc, and let slip the dogs of war . . ."

War in the streets. I go to a black market center where someone I am with can cash a check. Sheridan Square seems close enough but the cab, which travels at great speed, lets me off in Irving Place. I see a boat on a rack, and there is a whiff of the sea. I walk to Fisherman's Wharf. On a corner. I can see the water right at my feet, deep and clear and blue. I am bloody and dirty. Walking with a staff, trying to find my way home. Also junk-sick. I have some junk at home, if I can ever find my way there.

In a strange apartment. I am in bed, the bedroom door is open and there is a light in the next room. The light goes out. I get out of bed, gun in hand. The front room faces the street. I can see that the ceiling light is out. There are people passing outside. In a corner is a table with some meaningless pieces of equipment that I know to be nuclear-related. Looks like an old construction set, or the wreck of the KANU radio tower. Ian has gone out to a gay bar. It is 5:00 a.m. and I decide he has slept overnight someplace. Back in the bedroom, I notice that I am wearing gray suede gloves that would make it difficult to fire the gun double action.

In a cyanide chamber with several other condemned prisoners. We are lying on metal couches with holes in the metal—mesh, in fact. Now the executioner, who is a dwarf or at least legless, brings in the cyanide eggs and I can smell the cyanide. There is a sink with some water at one end of the room. I am there with another prisoner, perhaps we can save ourselves by putting our faces underwater. How long before the doors will be opened?

I was in Tangier in a bar and Hemingway was there. There are stone steps going down to the sea, steps of some reddish-brown stone. Ten thousand years, and what will remain?

The Land of the Dead. Two a.m. in Paris. The room I occupy is small and narrow but not rectangular. Straight on one side with a small window, the other wall comes in at an angle. Like the rooms in the film *Brazil*. There is another person in the room . . . a boy dressed only in black shorts. He has black hair and pale white skin. I am lying on the floor, then he straddles me, looking at my face in an appraising manner. His appraisal is not sexual. He has the appearance of a male nurse or orderly, someone connected to a hospital. He says something about "the Maintenance Ward" or "the Main Ward." I interpret this as an indication he is trying to decide to which ward I will be assigned.

Shift to Hong Kong. Paul Lund, deceased, explains to me about "toweling heroin." One covers one's head with a towel and sniffs it. Seems there is at present a crackdown. A girl who talked too much to the wrong people has been taken for a one-way ride. I point out this is not a Western city. I say: "Such indiscretion is difficult to condone," adding: "These things happen."

Little parachutes raining down, like the kind I used to make from a handkerchief, maybe fifty or a hundred of these parachutes, from the top of a high building.

A feeling of freedom. A breakthrough. I am going south to live in a shack, in a swamp, maybe. It's all quite magical.

A man is trying to sell me beach frontage in Mexico.

An awful *pension* where there are four beds in a corridor. The whole place is littered with ratty old furniture and tippy tables. I want breakfast and there is what looks like a dining room, with glasses of water on a table and one glass of orange juice. Talking to an old mobster who says he has avoided trouble and stayed alive by keeping himself in the background. There is a scar on his face, which is rather round in contour, with close-cropped black hair. He looks like an old fighter, or fight manager. The Indians are coming.

"Calling all butchers."

I am running now, without hope of getting away. I am by a swimming pool, very dirty, full of stagnant water, with sticks and algae. Someone shoots me in the back with a long bamboo arrow. I am dying . . . spitting blood by the pool. James is there.

Another dream, before or after. I am in bed, spitting blood into the pillow. Mother is there. I say: "I am dying."

In the house at Price Road. Dark inside the house. Heavy palpable darkness of danger. I go down to the living room. Here and there are plates of glass with wedges bitten out. Where is Mort? Lucien eating glass on Bedford Street in the Village. Where is Mort? I open the front door, outside is daylight but it is night inside. Something contrived about the daylight, as if it is just a special little patch of light that might go out at any moment. When I open the front door Mother is there, very young and smart, in 1920s style, like *The Green Hat*.

I make up a bed in the living room over by the French doors that overlook the terrace and the garden. I am putting pillows together, like a Pullman berth. There is a boy in the berth with me. His arms are tanned and there are needle marks at the elbow. We start to make it, in a vague groping way. Attention is focused on his arm, the underside, at the elbow.

Many years ago my first contact with the Land of the Dead: It is in the backyard of 4664 Pershing Avenue. Darkness and patches of oil and smell of oil. In the house now, and I am bending over Mother from in front, eating her back, like a dinosaur. Now Mother comes screaming into the room: "I had a terrible dream that you were eating my back." I have a long neck that reaches up and over her head. My face in the dream is wooden with horror. It is like a segment of film underexposed. Not enough light. The light is running out. Dinosaurs rise from the tar pits on La Brea Avenue. Oil and coal gas.

Silent motion in a transparent vehicle, or is it a vehicle? Then zero in on some detail, like the strange animal in winter rubble. This morning a pile of mortar and a part of a house wall. I know that this is in Madagascar. There is a steep slope down to the sea. The pile of rubble has been there for some time. It is compacted together. I see the Kaw River from my old studio window now. Back to the rubble, which is my point of entry—you will know a point of entry by the feeling . . . joy, hope, recognition!

"They fell down on their faces in land their own." Transcript of
Egyptian glyphs.

Mick Jagger is standing in an arched window. His arms out-
stretched like the diagram that NASA sent into space. He is very
thin. Seemed to be all right in some way. Running down towards a
subway entrance, I am barefoot and there is rough concrete and
wood, so I skim above the ground and off into the air at a flight of
steps. Can Mick do this? He seems to be still there.

Reminded of dream fragment with a Turkish bath full of hideously deformed pre-pubescent boys with deformed genitals and
swollen bodies, the genitals split at the end, swollen in the middle.
Thin as a pencil. The atmosphere is horrible and there are rooms
and levels and bunks full of them.

Nightmare of paralysis. Trying to call out. Reaching for gun with
numb finger, knowing that he cannot pull the trigger. What is happening here? Obviously the dreamer is helpless, in the possession
of any totally hostile invader. Is there something in bed with me?
Indeed there is—recall that a common hallucination of sensory dep-
rivation is the feeling of another body sprawled through one's own.

Wake from the nightmare in a strange room. Out the window I
can see people walking by a river. A chair catches my attention.
Where have I seen such a chair? The chair is the key here. The
heavy uncomfortable chair. Good only to hit someone over the head,
if his back is turned, or perhaps to ward off an attacking lion. At
least the chair is not flimsy.

Wake up finally into the real room in Lawrence, Kansas, at
3:00 a.m. Glance through the dream notes. A woman on phone says

she does not want *two* doctors. The set is clearly Venusian. Alien and distasteful.

Two sharp pictures. Walking by the Chase Manhattan Bank. See Mr. Bowles (not P. Bowles, but the Bowles who was an officer in the Chase Bank in London). This bank was held up by three people—one dressed as a woman, carrying a sawed-off shotgun. I arrived a few minutes after the robbery. Reading Laing's *The Divided Self*—on the breakfast table. Turn to story of David, an eighteen-year-old patient with a compulsion to act out female roles in front of a mirror. In the dream I see Bowles sitting at his desk in shirtsleeves, sleeves rolled up. He says one can retire on black market rates, that is, the *discrepancy* between official and black market rates.

I am going into space, and Mack Thomas is starting to fuck things up. Huncke is there, his face swollen and beaten. Jack Anderson is shocked when I refuse to support him any longer. Chewing gum in my mouth with a wad of leaves. Chimps eat the meat they bite and tear off their prey with wads of leaves. Murders in the rue Morgue. An orangutan shoves a woman up the chimney and cuts another woman's head off with a straight razor. The dream of two figures covered in pus-stained sheets. Chewing gum in recurrent dream. May refer to early sex trauma involving fellatio? A building twenty-two stories high, quite square, about thirty by thirty, made of yellow composition board, like the dorms outside of Boulder. An orange-squeezing machine. I can see my hand and arm when I point northwest. Look into the mirror and see a Negro face, but my hands on the basin are white.

The stream at Junction B. Streaked with iron. The dark figure of a chimp or gorilla in the dream and the big lemur that comes to my hand, the pinkish pig creature—some lemurs were the size of a large pig.

"Don't you want me? I am anybody to anybody who loves me."

"Are you Billy?" Stroking a large white cat. "Do you want me?"

In a strange apartment. I glimpse a black and white cat. Dad is trying to kill himself with my Snubbie. I am crying and saying "NO NO NO!"

Glimpse of an alien city towering into the sky, with copper roof cupolas and domes. Two miniature boys, about two feet high, were there and I told them I was an anthropologist. This seemed to please and reassure the boys, who proffered their tiny hands to shake. It was like they were reaching out through a medium I could not see. To say their hands were tiny is not definitive. They were hands from another sphere.

My sexual feelings, in human terms, seem to have withered away, or rather, to belong to a body and mind I no longer occupy. But I maintain an intense emotional feeling for animals. Imagine a *big lemur*. Lemur as big as I am, and cuddling up to me—nothing sexual, it's much more intense than that.

Driving across Paris in a taxi at breakneck speed, expecting a crash at any moment. A remote district of warehouses and empty streets.

We are going to visit Monsieur Genet. Up wide stairs in an old building, we come to his door, where we are met by a woman who escorts us in. Genet is seated at a table in a wheelchair. There are a number of people in the room, including what looks like an Arab policeman in uniform. Genet has a much larger face, of a strange yellow color. I tell him he is looking well.

We go into another room. It seems he wants my help in some way as a therapist. I am not at all sure I can be of any help. Now the party breaks up. I go with Genet to an apartment house. He will make a short visit with his editor. I say I will wait downstairs. A woman asks me if I will have coffee. I say yes and she brings me also a bottle of liqueur with gold flakes in it, that I can take back to America on the boat. I also have a Colt Python that someone has given me. How will I get it back through customs?

Now the editor comes downstairs. He is youngish, and dressed in a blue denim suit. He invites me upstairs, where I am offered Majoun in various pastries. Alan Ansen is there, Brion will come in another car. I eat several pastries.

Back through the sixties, slow letup in drug pressure . . . now back through the fifties . . . Anslinger in full swing. Morphine and Dilaudid scripts . . . Pantopon Rose . . . Old-time junkies at 103rd and Broadway . . . Back back clickety clack . . . Syrettes . . . World War II . . . The thirties . . . Heroin is $28 an ounce—back back . . . the Crash, the twenties . . . film stars on junk, Wally Read . . . Wilson Mizner . . . World War I . . . Keep the home fires burning though the hearts are yearning . . . back before the laws . . . another air . . . a different light . . . free lunch and beer at five cents a mug . . . back . . . no lines to the present . . . cut all lines . . . here come the lamplighters, ghostly private places . . . Westmoreland Place . . . Portland Place . . . empty houses, leaves blowing and drifting like shreds of time . . . radio silence on Portland Place . . . furtive seedy figures, rooming houses and chili parlors, hop joints, cathouses . . .

Arrive in Spain. There is just time to get off the boat, and the few disembarking passengers walk out into what looks like a very large living room, about the size of the Bunker, with shabby junk furniture.

Next thing: packing to leave. Seems there is a revolution, and we can hear shots in the distance. With Mort in a room with a shower. He says he wants to take a shower and I say, "I do, too," and start to take off my clothes and get a hard-on and almost go off when I wake up.

Night before last, a precognitive dream. A party or celebration, quite a few people present . . . James, Brion. Ian was there and we go into a bedroom in the house (which is not mine) to make it. But I can't get a coat and sweater off my arms . . .

Back to the party, there is a young man there with a beard. I see him quite clearly, about thirty . . . quiet, nice. Now in the bedroom I can see him outside a window. There is a partition between the bedroom and the other room where people are. The partition has a ragged hole in one corner, through which light enters with a garish cast in bright orange and black, unreal like a Halloween poster, the colors are too bright for life.

Last night went to John Myers' birthday party, and there is the young man with the beard I had seen in the dream. We talk about guns. Is he the one who killed the goose we eat? Number 2 shot, of course . . . a 12-gauge pump.

A dream about Wayne Propst, with a window behind him, partially melted, saying that we could invoke any political figures at our will and discretion. I admitted to seeing animals, kangaroos and giraffes, but the light must be turned down. I was petting a dog, and then there is a dog or other animal in my bed, with a pink head. I pick a flea off its head and crush the flea between my nails.

Afternoon Lake

July 27, 1991—after three weeks in the hospital in Topeka for triple bypass and fractured hip.

Flying over African set in a rickety old tin plane. I am in a windowless cubicle, jiggling about; if it turns upside down I will know this is It. But we land on the edge of a lake or inlet, in a basin. Standing there on the shore, I can see fish swimming in the clear, yellow water, twenty or thirty feet deep, and deeper towards the middle. Lily pads three feet across, yellow-gray in color, some dry on top—others soaked through, stems reaching down into the clear, still water. In the distance an inlet, in clear, golden afternoon light.

In that hospital there were interludes of blissful, painless tran-quillity. (I start awake with a cry of fear.) Slipping, falling, deeper and deeper into easeful rest after the perilous journey, silent peace by the afternoon lake where the sun never sets and it is always late afternoon.

How did we get here, somewhere in Africa? In a rickety old tin plane. He was in a metal-lined cubicle, sheet iron, like the inside of an orgone accumulator. There were no windows but it was light. He could feel the vibrations and he knew the plane was in danger of a crash, but it lands and he gets out.

He is on the edge of a lake, sixty feet deep in the middle. About two hundred yards across. On the other side is a village. Black children trickling out along the shore of the lake, in little white suits and dresses. The water is a clear yellow, slanting steeply down to the center. There are large lily pads three feet across, and the stems reaching down to the bottom in a green-yellow haze where big, black fish swim around the stems. Fish range from one foot to three feet in length. The lake is in a basin. Away in the distance in a golden glow, I can see more water, a larger lake or river.

I am standing on the near side of the basin with the pilot, who wears shorts and knee-length socks. He says something about the white stones that litter the slope, none larger than a Ping-Pong ball. I cannot see over the edge.

Slowly a familiar odor fills my nostrils. Piss? *Piss!!! The lake is piss.* Years and years of strong yellow piss. And slowly the full desolate horror of that stagnant place hits him like a kick in the stomach.

"Fishing, anyone?" The scales are encrusted with crystals of yellow piss, the flesh yellow and oily with piss. Where is the plane? No plane here. He tries to reach the top of the basin. Keeps sliding back on white stones, smooth and slippery. Where is the pilot? No pilot here. The sun is not moving. Just a steady glow in the golden distance, on the great brown-yellow river of shit and piss.

The Duad! Out of the basin!? Beyond the basin? There is nothing beyond the basin!

A deep slough of clear, yellow urine, seepage of centuries from the Duad, there in the western distance, bathed in the golden glow of a sun that never sets.

Eternal vigilance and skill in the use of weapons that will never be needed here in this yellow stalemate where it is always late afternoon.

— ᵔ ᵔ

In a classroom, like John Burroughs School. Room was crowded and I was in front room. Someone is paging Fred Turner. I say: "I know him and I will take the call and relay the message." The messenger is middle-aged, rather stout, dressed in some sort of gray uniform, mailman, janitor, doorman, messenger—and *not* a bearer of glad tidings.

Is Fred dead? The last I heard, he was in Argentina, teaching the Army how to win at Ping-Pong, a skill at which he excels. He must be about my age now—seventy-seven. I wonder if he still goes in for "minor incidents"? Just a *smudge*, you know. "Allah doesn't like that," in the mortal words of Beni Menisi. Still, the unfrocked Captain had a way of not being there when it went down.

"Oh yoo hooo?"

They are drumming him out of the Service. They have moved him out to a tiny outhouse and given all the NCOs instructions not to obey his orders, if any. *And* they have called a Z Board on him. And some colonel, like carved in rock at Mount Rushmore, takes out his pipe and grates:

"So far as we are concerned, Turner, you are no goddamned good to the Army."

Oh boy, could he go into his naive little-boy act.

"I'm sorry to hear you say that, sir. I've always tried to do my job, sir, to the best of my ability, sir. Can you cite any specific derelictions, sir? I've worked hard for this rank, sir. Why, I remember when I got my bars as a Second Louie, and how I used to choke up on that song: 'Bars on your shoulders, And stars in your eyes.' "

He's got no shame. He bellows it out with "The Star-Spangled Banner" out the other side of his wide mouth—it's one of those mouths that go out above and beyond the perimeter.

"Has this man had a psychiatric evaluation?" the Old Pipe grates.

So sitting out there in his outhouse.

"You can't beat the Z Board, Fred," they all tell him. "Last man that tried went out in a straitjacket."

So at this critical junction, Captain Fred wins a Chrysler Town and Country in a contest, for his Army slogan:

"Preparedness in peace. Preponderance in war."

And Fred drives out, waving and blowing his horn and pulling the disintegrating outhouse behind him on a tow chain. Everybody turns out to see it, and right in front of the Officers' Club he drops the outhouse, which pops open with a prerecorded Bronx cheer:

"Adios and toodle-oo!"

But I guess everybody's number comes up sooner or later. Been tapped myself twice now, three times, by that parchment-faced messenger. The postman who always rings twice.

In Paris, a cheap hotel. Room 197, right next to the toilet. Thin walls. A cubicle room with a narrow lumpy bed. One chair, a wardrobe with no door on it. A small desk. Outside I can see French signs. Advertisements. French. French. French. A terrible feeling of desolation and boredom and emptiness. Like there is nothing outside but the French words. I walk out, being sure to remember where the hotel is.

I need to change some money. It is a quarter to five, and the change booths close at five. I ask a woman in an open shop, *"Où est un bureau de change?"* She says she can change some American money for me. I have two very large notes in my trouser pocket, of a rust-brown color. One will be enough, in case the woman at the hotel wants to be paid in advance. I have no luggage with me. The area adjacent to the hotel looks like an airport.

Antony and Brion are there and they try to cheer me up. Brion

tells me about something he calls "dream sheets" that he kept as
a child.

The city is vaguely reminiscent of New York, with the Land of the
Dead superimposed. Dark, dirty streets littered with trash and garbage, but trash from what usage? And garbage from what foods and
what containers? The smell of death and rot is here, from decay of
unfamiliar offal. Many of the buildings appear deserted or semi-
deserted. Many have stained marble facades and steps. The streets
are narrow. A park in front of the traveler is a twisted tangle of
roots and vines and misshapen trees.

I am leaving an old lover, who has taken a wife and has no
further need of me. Looking at the tangled roots, the rotting fruit
and phosphorescent excrement, I realize that I must face the nature
of my own need.

Why do I need to be needed, and why can I not face and elim-
inate this abject need? For inexplicable and therefore inordinate
need is always abject and unsightly. A man who suffers, however
intensely, from frustrated sexual needs is always an object of contempt. He has only himself to blame. But it may be very difficult
for him to face the parts of himself he can blame.

The pain of thinking about the lost lover and his new lover dis-
porting themselves, with no thought of my pain and need, cuts like
a salted wire whip.

When you unsaid the day and split the hour
I thought, What do seconds do after hours?
And I thought, Minutes are here to go.
So told Edgar Allan Poe

In a brief time before the dead eons
blamed the live months for nothing and everything
But nobody and nothing could heal the split
as time blubbered like severed coral
And there was no time left to mend
the wounds of punctured time spilling
into the void of used razor blades in
the heart of bellowing Texas
For theirs is not an ill for mending
Better take it to the waves that
soothe the Band-Aids of rainy afternoons
And consummate the spray paint's despairing
flares across the tilted ponds of
Despond and mercurial pollutions
For there is no balm in suburbia
for the lost bougainvillea's purple lament
For it was after all present and pre-
written eons ago with a broken stone hoe
bowed by the weight of centuries he stands
and offers to you his pre-callused
hands that mar the bubble gum's
affreuse, frivolity, with false teeth
in a screaming skull, molten lead
in the screaming ear and brittle
nuance of greasy fear. It is not
too late to turn the page.

I am waiting for Paul Klein, of the Klein Gallery in Chicago, to
come and select pictures for an upcoming show. The doorbell rings.
I open the door. A man stands there on the rubber mat with "Wel-

come" embossed on it. I motion him in. I motion him to an armchair, in imitation green leather, quite comfortable, purchased for five dollars at a yard sale. I sit a few feet away, at a round table, with a lamp that is always lighted. He comes over and sits at the table.

"I want to be *near* you," he says.

He has a shabby briefcase with him, and he extracts some pamphlets. All I can remember about the pamphlets is that certain phrases are in a larger and darker typeface than the others. But no one word remains, and I was never able to find the pamphlet that he left when I gave him two dollars. (There used to be two-dollar bills.) Nor can I remember anything about the man except his nearness, which he left behind. He was neither fat nor thin—young nor old. The only impression is a gray presence.

Klein and his wife arrived shortly, and made selections.

I went to the opening, at which three pictures were sold.

Back in Lawrence in my two-bedroom house, I am making notes on an index card. I have written, "Yves Klein sometimes set his canvases on fire" (I have done this too, with wood pieces, and sometimes with good results), when James arrives and tells me the Klein Gallery, in fact the whole block where the gallery was located, has burned to the ground. No implication that Klein had anything to do with the fire.

It is to be remembered that Yves is not exactly a name, but rather an appellation, like "Mister." *Any* Klein, any little person could have twiddled with wires, thrown a cigarette (not quite out) in a wastebasket. He got there first. A cat escaped from the fire and was named Fireball, and carried home by a passing stranger.

Unthinkable that these events are in any way connected?

The greasy, treacherous General, belching garlic through gold teeth. And the slender aristocrat, who cultivates a Machiavellian image.

"You are the best soldier I have ever bought, but you have not learned to obey orders."

"Depends on the orders."

"No it *does not* depend on the orders, or on any other consideration. For example, I say: 'Go and cut the prick off Captain Hernández and bring it to me in a matchbox so I can show my whore wife how small her lover's prick has become . . .' "

"I am not paid for such services."

"Suppose the pay was very good."

"No amount of pay could compensate."

"So? What a man would not do, for any amount of money or other commodities such as power and time, is a measure of his worth. And a man of such worth is always highly dangerous."

"You have a reason to doubt my loyalty?"

"Oh, no. It is precisely the loyalty, the principle, that makes you dangerous."

A race without stomachs, but some of them sport auxiliary stomachs. Relieved of nutrient functions, they carry the culinary arts to refinements that have not been seen since Roman days . . . marry the liver of the fugu fish to the kidney of the Brazilian fruit-eating fish. And—once the poison glands are removed—the tiny blue-ringed octopus. A carefully balanced diet, leaves no residue like a careless cartilage . . . so the rectum, relieved of excretion, is freed for recreational purposes. Or, it can be surgically removed at any time.

Such meals can cost upwards of $5,000 per person, and certain *special dishes* can cost $20,000 a portion. Need I say more? *Dare* I say more?

(The most deadly picture is a picture of nothing at all. The colors are there, and the contrasts, but there is no image, nothing. One searches desperately for some face, some tree, some house, and there is nothing.)

Walking along a raised sidewalk, I open a door that leads into a private apartment, trying to find my way through to the corridor beyond, which is a public thoroughfare. Having dinner with L. Ron Hubbard. One has to walk up a steep stairway to the dining area. He is wearing a double-breasted vest and wide mauve tie. He is very composed and decorous.

I have a dental appointment with Jock Jardine. My appointment was for two, and it is now two forty-five. Meet Mary McCarthy in the U.S. Consulate and tell her she is looking well, which is a lie, she looks terrible. Lined up at a cashier's window to cash checks, actually I have no checks.

"After such knowledge what forgiveness?" Eliot.

The Tree of Knowledge? The Tree of Knowledge will inevitably confer on mortals to know the mind of God. In time. Checkmate. Three thousand years from now. So God had to play his trump card. The Atom Bomb. But was it not Satan who enticed Eve into eating Adam's apple and got them both evicted? Satan miscalculated, or he would not have lost the battle. And now God, like Kali, must resort to Satan's weapon of total destruction. He also miscalculated. He did not foresee the intervention of the Visitors. Result: total confusion. Is this Satan pretending to be God, or God pretending to be Satan? It is both, more or less, depending on the viewpoint, which shifts from millisecond to millisecond.

I get in the elevator. Two elevators opposite each other. I am not sure which elevator goes to the CIA office, or is it both? Get in the elevator to my right, and press a button for the sixth floor.

Get off at reception desk. A new girl at the desk. She hands me a card on which to state the nature of my business, and tells me to wait. *Me to wait!!??*

"I am William Burroughs. I don't have to wait for anybody!"

Confused mutterings. Clearly there have been some changes here. She leads me to a small office, carpeted in brown. One desk. One chair.

"Mr. Ferguson is on his way."

Now I am getting danger signals, loud and clear. Try the door through which I came in. Locked. Expecting at any second the hiss of poison gas. I try another door at the end of a very short hall, like a closet. Metal handle of curved configuration. Open.

I walk out now through a maze of rooms and corridors. Elevators here and there. "Why, they don't know who I am." And who are you? The Director of Directors. Someone didn't want me to see who was in his room. Pick up what looks like an unfinished weapon. A tube with cylinder attached at one end.

Now, when I was four or five years old, I had a little gold knife and I used to suck it for the steel taste. Folded, of course—thé puckering, steely taste. Ended up swallowing the knife—but let that pass (as it did, three days later.) Well, in any case, this metal taste in the mouth was the first sign of the disease.

The Metal Sickness, or the Steels. It tasted great at first, then it got to be too good, and then it began to hurt and ache, and sores covered the gums and tongue, that which oozed out what looked like mercury or melted solder, and one doctor said it smelled like rotten solder would smell, if solder could rot, right down to the bleeding bone. The teeth and gums and tongue went first, then the throat and nose. Next the case is shitting out bloody solder with pieces of intestine, and puking up his phosphorescent guts. Disease ran its course in about three days or less.

Set is Harry's Hafen Museum in Hamburg. This occupies four stories of junk, accumulated by Harry over many years, from sailors and visitors. Seashells, knives, masks, pictures, books, magazines, crystals, stuffed animals, from rats to bears and camels, stray cats shitting through the shelves, up and down stairways and ramps chasing mice and rats that gnaw on the exhibits. A pervasive stink of cat and mouse urine and excrement, decaying animals, that seeps into one's clothes. Everything is for sale, if anyone wants to buy it.

In dream, a long bar of rusty sheet tin runs along the front of the museum inside the entrance. James and I standing at the bar. We are elbowed down to the end of the bar by a brash young Cockney. (The bar is otherwise empty.) I finally pull a .32 APC Colt Pocket Model 1903, and stick it under his nose. He makes cockney noises of confusion and defeat: "Uh—ah—different rules—" and sidles away.

James and I are on our way to a play called *The Gray Guild*. Graham Greene? Along the front of the museum, doors of rusty dented metal, pocked with fissures and holes. Outside, cockney boys beat on the door, clamoring to get in. James and I leave and a crowd of East End trash bursts in.

I read a tabloid called *The Weekly World News,* which often pro-
vides me with material. Here is an example:

"EARTH IS FALLING OUT OF ORBIT. Soviet scientist predicts
planet will spin out of the solar system by the year 2000 . . ."

This reminds me of a dream recounted by Paul Bowles: "People
were rushing through the streets, screaming *'Off the track! Off the
track!'*—and there was no hope at all."

Paul is not given to relating his dreams. This is the only case
that I can recall.

Cabin on the Lake

Now I got no use for a big house, just two bedrooms, and one is my
art studio . . . don't really want a guest room, 'cause I don't really
want guests, they can sleep on the sofa . . . and I got me this cabin
out on the lake. Got it cheap since I was able to put up cash, which
the owners needed to put down on another house they is buying out
in the country. Could easy sell it now, but what for? A few thousand
profit? Nowadays what can you do with that kinda money?

My neighbor tells me right in front of my dock (I've got the *access,*
and that is the thing matters here on the lake . . . a dock, see?),
well, my neighbor tells me that right in front of my dock is the best
catfish fishing in the lake, but I don't want to catch a catfish. They
squawk when you pull them out of the water and snap at you like
an animal, and I don't want to kill no animal. Besides which, they
is a bitch to clean . . . have to skin them with a pair of pliers, and
their guts is like animal guts. Course, I could turn the fish loose—
unless he swallowed the hook, and then what I'd have to do is cut
his head clean off with a machete and end his misery.

I could cope with a bass, or better, some bluegills—half pound
is as tasty a fish as a man can eat—fresh from the lake, and I got

me an aluminum flat-bottom boat, ten foot long, $270 . . . a real
bargain. I likes to row out in the middle of the lake and just let the
boat drift. I hear tell there's been flying saucers sighted out here
on the lake, and I'm hoping maybe one will pick me up. These
aliens the government is trying to hush up, they got no stomachs,
nourish themselves from photosynthesis—so you can see why the
scum on top of us want to hack that up. The whole fucking planet
is built on eating, and if a surgical intervention could remove all
stomachs, the whole shithouse would come crashing down and then
we could look at Bush and that tight-assed bitch Thatcher and
Mohamad Mahathir, that Malaysian bastard hangs people for smoking pot . . . would be flopping around like displaced catfish, only I
wouldn't feel a thing for them, just stand there and watch them die.
It would be my pleasure.

So I rows out and lets the boat drift, looking at the hill beyond
the lake and just hoping for a flying saucer and humming to myself,
"Swing low, sweet chariot, coming for to carry me home," and take
out my stomach so I don't give a shit about no government. I can
just set there from here on out . . . but nothing happens, leastwise
nothing I can *feel* happening . . . but maybe it will happen when I
go to sleep . . . but then I just wake up in my bed, to get up and
feed my six cats. First thing would be to have their stomachs took
out, so they would let up aggravating me.

Now lying comes as natural as breathing to a politician, and just
as necessary for his survival. I reckon that's what happened with
John F. Kennedy . . . he was on the edge of committing the criminal,
unforgivable sin: he was about to tell the truth, and somebody called
a special number in Washington.

Yeah, it sure would pleasure me to see the whole lot of them—
Bennett, Bush, Thatcher, Mohamad Mahathir, Sad-Ass Hussein—
flopping around out of their medium and gasping out their last lies.

One thing I hate more than other things is a liar. Maybe it's because I am not capable of lying. Even a simple everyday lie, like claiming I am sick to avoid a trip or an appointment, rings so hollow, even over the phone, that nobody will buy it.

Breakfast Eggs

It was a good day when he could eat two boiled eggs. An egg has got to be just right. One little bit of off taste, and his weak appetite would falter . . . like this morning, the first egg was all right but there was something just a shade wrong about the second. Maybe he would eat it later. Maybe with the remains of the toast, unless the cats got up on the table and licked at the butter.

Last night I was in Switzerland, and there on a hillside was a lion crouched over a man who looked dead . . . and there was a bank in front of me, which was in ruins, with the door stuck open, and I go in and try to close the door to keep the lion out, but the door won't close. Somebody is with me and the floor of the bank is littered with plaster, holes and ditches here and there, full of dust, and we find a bar of a metal called selenium, which is more valuable than platinum, even got some special properties. The metal is an orange-red-brown color I use a lot in painting.

I once visited a hunting baron in Switzerland with horns sticking out all over the walls, and a gun room. He had a Nagant gas-seal revolver I'd never actually seen before, only pictures. Later when he serves us coffee and some terrible sweet caramel cake, he tells about shooting a cat on his property and said: "I like to shoot cats."

At that time I was not a devoted cat lover like now, and I regret ever since not telling him: ". . . devoted cat lover myself. Hmmmm, I think we have an *urgent* appointment." So this is a clear wish fulfillment, and he is the man under the lion, which is the way I would like to see him. These trophy hunters deserve what they get.

Later there was a party full of young boys, and Allen Ginsberg is presiding. Everyone is smoking pot, and I hope we don't get raided. Then I am in a strange city and out of junk . . . could I hit this doctor I know for an Rx? Probably not . . . or go to the local methadone clinic which, as I remember, is on the seventeenth floor of an office building.

Now an egg just borders on the disgusting any way you open it. A week ago, I open an egg and out plops a bright red embryonic chicken into the pan, and ever since then, I boil my eggs and also hold them up to the light. You can tell if there is anything wrong when the light shines through.

Rien ne va plus. Round and round the little ball goes.

Ich sterbe. They were drafted. A few chickens. It's the only way to live . . . a fertile egg to keep it from happening.

Glass . . . ass.

Bottle . . . Aristotle.

"He's got it on the Greek."

Cockney rhyming slang, to indicate the mark's wallet is in his hip pocket. Now isn't that funny? The mark doesn't think so. He thinks he's lucky to get out of there with his ass in one piece.

The calico cat licks the toast crust on the blue plate (all calicos are female . . . almost all), savoring the salt and butter. I move half-eaten boiled eggs (two) out of her reach.

I will brown fresh toast later, to eat with the eggs . . . hoarding scraps of hunger.

An old man's hunger is precious.

I was woken up by an explosion behind my buttocks. An explosion *from without.* Wake up in my room and bed, very much frightened, trying to hold myself in readiness for some hostile attack. But I don't know where the attack will come from, or how to defend myself. Probably (I decide) by getting out of any defensive position. I know somehow that the gun always by my hand—Smith & Wesson .38 Special—will be of no use.

Then I wake up. Fear is gone, and threat gone. What and why? Then I remember that I have recently read about Willy Bioff, who testified in a probe into extortion perpetrated by the filmmakers' union. Willy was the enforcer in this shakedown, and he bought himself out by testifying against such notables as Frank Nitti ("The Waiter"), Cherry Nose Gio, and others of the same caliber. For ten years he lived happily in Phoenix under the name of Nelson. Then one morning he climbed into his pickup truck and tapped the starter with his short, thick legs, which came to rest on the lawn some distance from what remained of the truck and Willy Bioff.

But I am not Willy Bioff, despite the same initials . . . why somebody put a bomb under my ass? Seems that somebody or something draws some sort of analogy. I guess we are all guilty of everything.

A number of dreams involving travel at high speed under dangerous conditions, usually by car. In these dreams I am *physically frightened*. Someone else is always driving. In cars, the driver is my father. Refers, I assume, to the desperate race of the spermatozoa to penetrate the waiting egg.

A road cut through heavy second-growth timber, the road structured from split logs, split side down, nailed to a framework. Looking north, the trees are flush with the road on the left side, and seem to have been shaved with an axe. Ahead there is a clearing.

Location is northern Canada, Alaska, Siberia; there is a lake ahead. It is raining and there is water in puddles beside the road and ahead of us.

I am in a car and my father is driving. I seem to be lying down with my head behind my father's shoulders. Such roads, slicked over with wet clay, are slippery as greased glass, and I say from the backseat:

"Dad! Please slow down!"

Dream years ago: in a car, pinwheeling off the road, and I am out of my body with no pain, floating above the wreck.

It was a Thursday. For me, a portentous conjunction: I was born February 5, 1914, which was a Thursday. September 17 is also a special date for me. Arbitrary but significant, with potential for good or bad luck.

It was 8:00 a.m. when I left my house in Lawrence, with Michael Emerton driving his BMW. The rain is coming down in sheets, and there is a yellow-gray haze across the sky. We pass the toll booth and the quarry lake, going 65 m.p.h. Then the rain comes down so heavy and visibility is limited to the hood of the BMW and I *know* and start to say, "For Christ's sake, Michael, slow down and pull over," when the car aquaplanes and slams into the guard-rail and skids across the highway and into the ditch. *Stop!*

For a moment I can't move, and I mutter, "I need an ambulance," as if my need can conjure up such a contrivance. Then the door opens and a young man in a brown windbreaker says, "Can you walk?"

I find that I can indeed walk, with my cane and his supporting arm.

"Better move away," he says; "the car might catch fire." Another young man is helping Michael. They drive us ahead to the truckstop.

"You guys are lucky you're not dead."

Lawrence Journal-World, Sept. 22, 1992; Classified Ads

Card of Thanks

To express our heartfelt thanks to the two young motorists who helped us out of a wrecked BMW 6 mi. E. of Lawrence on turnpike on Thurs., Sept. 17, 1992.

William Burroughs & Michael Emerton

Michael B. Emerton shot himself November 4, 1992.

An experience most deeply felt is the most difficult to convey in words. Remembering brings the emptiness, the acutely painful awareness of irreparable loss.

From my window, I can see the marble slab over Ruski's grave . . . Ruski, my first and always special cat, a Russian Blue from the woods of East Kansas. Every time I see the grave, I get that empty feeling where something was, and isn't anymore, and will never be again.

Michael Emerton   **August 1985, aged nineteen**

In the 1920s there were stage shows between the films. I hated these for the most part, they went on and on and I just wanted to see the movies. I remember now an occasion, I was with my father, a big rawboned performer got up and sang:

Sailing on
Sailing on
I am sailing on.

That was sixty-odd years ago. Where was he sailing to? I can't remember the film but I can see him quite clearly from here. Not a young man, early to mid-forties, tall, angular, awkward, thick red wrists, his sleeves too short, worn blue serge suit . . .

What did my father say after the show? "Big rawboned fellow . . ."

The full misery of the human condition hits me when I think about that long-ago singer.

I remember a story by de Maupassant, "La Vie," can't quote exactly. Traveler stops in a deep gorge in the mountains of Corsica to ask directions at a farmhouse. A rushing stream, already dark in the late afternoon, the valley is so deep. And this woman who came from Paris, a good family, had married a Corsican and lived in this valley for forty years. "A feeling of desolation and horror swept through me at the thought of forty years in this remote dark valley. The frightful misery of the human condition, cradled in dreams until death."

A great surge of confidence, like a high wind shaking an iron tree. I am in some corridor like an airport. *I am taking over now.* At my feet are two little boys, one slightly older than the other, about eight. I pass them some rice and the older one grabs my hand and I can't shake him loose.

Remember my own early childhood: "When I grow up I will put a stop to this disgusting spit in my mouth. I will find a way. *I will go round the world.* And the snot in my nose, too. *I will go round the world."*

I am in a train at night, in my lower berth. The train is going very fast, I can tell by the way it shakes rattles and rolls. I have much fear of crashing. The train must be going ninety miles per hour.

"Oh well," I tell myself, "the engineer must know what he is doing."

"Not necessarily."

We are coming to the English frontier, and there will be a customs inspection. There is a paper of heroin hidden in my terry-cloth bathrobe. If it is found, I will plead with the inspector for a chance to *finish my education.*

Last night dream that paper horizon. The heroin looked at empty April. What is grief? The immediate look at a cat calendar . . . empty afternoon. Michael shot himself, delete "Why?" from your mind, which I never used, thick and gummy with dust. The planet is dying. Overhead lights sputtered out like an old joke. This old actor, see? Who was me, see? Real permanent, black and white. This you gotta hear. This old actor, see? Who *are* you? Somebody who committed suicide. People I have known. I don't know any details. Loft on Franklin Street, sleeping pills.

Leafing through old index cards. Mother in a packing crate. She has cancer. Frozen? To be checked through to Salt Lake River.

There is a change . . . Can I get it all straight?